The Wanderer's Necklace

Book II Byzantium

by

H. Rider Haggard

Double9
BOOKS

The Wanderer's Necklace
Book II Byzantium
by H. Rider Haggard

ISBN: 978-93-68095-85-9

Published by

DOUBLE 9 BOOKS
2/13-B, Ansari Road
Daryaganj, New Delhi – 110002
info@double9books.com
www.double9books.com
Tel. 011-40042856

ABOUT THE AUTHOR

H. Rider Haggard's high-quality known for his works that mix factors of journey, exploration, and the supernatural. Haggard's writing fashion and bright creativeness earned him a lasting region inside the global of traditional literature. One of his lesser-recognized works is "A Yellow God," this novella is a departure from Haggard's greater famous titles like "She" and "King Solomon's Mines," delving right into a darker and greater supernatural realm. "A Yellow God" is ready in South Africa and tells the tale of brothers, John and James, who end up entangled in a mysterious and lethal quest. The novella unfolds with a haunting environment, weaving topics of greed, energy, and the supernatural. The narrative explores the magical and enigmatic, as the brothers confront a chain of supernatural activities and dark forces. Haggard's storytelling mastery is clear inside the way he combines adventure and the eerie to create a unique narrative enjoy. While "A Yellow God" won't be as widely identified as a number of his other works, it showcases H. Rider Haggard's versatility as a creator, providing a one-of-a-kind measurement of his literary expertise.

CONTENTS

CHAPTER I
IRENE, EMPRESS OF THE EARTH

A gulf of blackness and the curtain lifts again upon a very different Olaf from the young northern lord who parted from Iduna at the place of sacrifice at Aar.

I see myself standing upon a terrace that overlooks a stretch of quiet water, which I now know was the Bosphorus. Behind me are a great palace and the lights of a vast city; in front, upon the sea and upon the farther shore, are other lights. The moon shines bright above me, and, having naught else to do, I study my reflection in my own burnished shield. It shows a man of early middle life; he may be thirty or five-and-thirty years of age; the same Olaf, yet much changed. For now my frame is tall and well-knit, though still somewhat slender; my face is bronzed by southern suns; I wear a short beard; there is a scar across my cheek, got in some battle; my eyes are quiet, and have lost the first liveliness of youth. I know that I am the captain of the Northern Guard of the Empress Irene, widow of the dead emperor, Leo the Fourth, and joint ruler of the Eastern Empire with her young son, Constantine, the sixth of that name.

How I came to fill this place, however, I do not know. The story of my journey from Jutland to Byzantium is lost to me. Doubtless it must have taken years, and after these more years of humble service, before I rose to be the captain of Irene's Northern Guard that she kept ever about her person, because she would not trust her Grecian soldiers.

My armour was very rich, yet I noted about myself two things that were with me in my youth. One was the necklace of golden shells, divided from each other by beetles of emeralds, that I had taken from the Wanderer's grave at Aar, and the other the cross-hilted bronze sword with which this same Wanderer had been girded in his grave. I know now that because of this weapon, which was of a metal and shape strange to that land, I had the byname of Olaf Red-Sword, and I know also that none wished to feel the weight of this same ancient blade.

When I had finished looking at myself in the shield, I leaned upon the parapet staring at the sea and wondering how the plains of Aar looked that night beneath this selfsame moon, and whether Freydisa were dead by now, and whom Iduna had married, and if she ever thought of me, or if Steinar came to haunt her sleep.

So I mused, till presently I felt a light touch upon my shoulder, and swung round to find myself face to face with the Empress Irene herself.

"Augusta!" I said, saluting, for, as Empress, that was her Roman title, even though she was a Greek.

"You guard me well, friend Olaf," she said, with a little laugh. "Why, any enemy, and Christ knows I have plenty, could have cut you down before ever you knew that he was there."

"Not so, Augusta," I answered, for I could speak their Greek tongue well; "since at the end of the terrace the guards stand night and day, men of my own blood who can be trusted. Nothing which does not fly could gain this place save through your own chambers, that are also guarded. It is not usual for any watch to be set here, still I came myself in case the Empress might need me."

"That is kind of you, my Captain Olaf, and I think I do need you. At least, I cannot sleep in this heat, and I am weary of the thoughts of State, for many matters trouble me just now. Come, change my mind, if you can, for if so I'll thank you. Tell me of yourself when you were young. Why did you leave your northern home, where I've heard you were a barbarian chief, and wander hither to Byzantium?"

"Because of a woman," I answered.

"Ah!" she said, clapping her hands; "I knew it. Tell me of this woman whom you love."

"The story is short, Augusta. She bewitched my foster-brother, and caused him to be sacrificed to the northern gods as a troth-breaker, and I do not love her."

"You'd not admit it if you did, Olaf. Was she beautiful, well, say as I am?"

I turned and looked at the Empress, studying her from head to foot. She was shorter than Iduna by some inches, also older, and therefore of a thicker build; but, being a fair Greek, her colour was much the same, save that the eyes were darker. The mouth, too, was more hard. For the rest, she was a royal-looking and lovely woman in the flower of her age, and splendidly attired in robes broidered with gold, over which she wore long strings of rounded pearls. Her rippling golden hair was dressed in the old Greek fashion, tied in a simple knot behind her head, and over it was thrown a light veil worked with golden stars.

"Well, Captain Olaf," she said, "have you finished weighing my poor looks against those of this northern girl in the scales of your judgment? If so, which of us tips the beam?"

"Iduna was more beautiful than ever you can have been, Augusta," I replied quietly.

She stared at me till her eyes grew quite round, then puckered up her mouth as though to say something furious, and finally burst out laughing.

"By every saint in Byzantium," she said, "or, rather, by their relics, for of live ones there are none, you are the strangest man whom I have known. Are you weary of life that you dare to say such a thing to me, the Empress Irene?"

"Am I weary of life? Well, Augusta, on the whole I think I am. It seems to me that death and after it may interest us more. For the rest, you asked me a question, and, after the fashion of my people, I answered it as truthfully as I could."

"By my head, you have said it again," she exclaimed. "Have you not heard, most innocent Northman, that there are truths which should not be mentioned and much less repeated?"

"I have heard many things in Byzantium, Augusta, but I pay no attention to any of them—or, indeed, to little except my duty."

"Now that this, this—what's the girl's name?"

"Iduna the Fair," I said.

"——this Iduna has thrown you over, at which I am sure I do not wonder, what mistresses have you in Byzantium, Olaf the Dane?"

"None at all," I answered. "Women are pleasant, but one may buy sweets too dear, and all that ever I saw put together were not worth my brother Steinar, who lost his life through one of them."

"Tell me, Captain Olaf, are you a secret member of this new society of hermits of which they talk so much, who, if they see a woman, must hold their faces in the sand for five minutes afterwards?"

"I never heard of them, Augusta."

"Are you a Christian?"

"No; I am considering that religion—or rather its followers."

"Are you a pagan, then?"

"No. I fought a duel with the god Odin, and cut his head off with this sword, and that is why I left the North, where they worship Odin."

"Then what are you?" she said, stamping her foot in exasperation.

"I am the captain of your Imperial Majesty's private guard, a little of a philosopher, and a fair poet in my own language, not in Greek. Also, I can play the harp."

"You say 'not in Greek,' for fear lest I should ask you to write verses to me, which, indeed, I shall never do, Olaf. A soldier, a poet, a philosopher, a harpist, one who has renounced women! Now, why have you renounced women, which is unnatural in a man who is not a monk? It must be because you still love this Iduna, and hope to get her some day."

I shook my head and answered,

"I might have done that long ago, Augusta."

"Then it must be because there is some other woman whom you wish to gain. Why do you always wear that strange necklace?" she added sharply. "Did it belong to this savage girl Iduna, as, from the look of it, it might well have done?"

"Not so, Augusta. She took it for a while, and it brought sorrow on her, as it will do on all women save one who may or may not live to-day."

"Give it me. I have taken a fancy to it; it is unusual. Oh! fear not, you shall receive its value."

"If you wish the necklace, Augusta, you must take the head as well; and my counsel to you is that you do neither, since they will bring you no good luck."

"In truth, Captain Olaf, you anger me with your riddles. What do you mean about this necklace?"

"I mean, Augusta, that I took it from a very ancient grave——"

"That I can believe, for the jeweller who made it worked in old Egypt," she interrupted.

"——and thereafter I dreamed a dream," I went on, "of the woman who wears the other half of it. I have not seen her yet, but when I do I shall know her at once."

"So!" she exclaimed, "did I not tell you that, east or west or north or south, there *is* some other woman?"

"There was once, Augusta, quite a thousand years ago or more, and there may be again now, or a thousand years hence. That is what I am trying to find out. You say the work is Egyptian. Augusta, at your convenience, will you be pleased to make another captain in my place? I would visit Egypt."

"If you leave Byzantium without express permission under my own hand—not the Emperor's or anybody else's hand; mine, I say—and are caught, your eyes shall be put out as a deserter!" she said savagely.

"As the Augusta pleases," I answered, saluting.

"Olaf," she went on in a more gentle voice, "you are clearly mad; but, to tell truth, you are also a madman who pleases me, since I weary of the rogues and lick-spittles who call themselves sane in Byzantium. Why, there's not a man in all the city who would dare to speak to me as you have spoken to-night, and like that breeze from the sea, it is refreshing. Lend me that necklace, Olaf, till to-morrow morning. I want to examine it in the lamplight, and I swear to you that I will not take it from you or play you any tricks about it."

"Will you promise not to wear it, Augusta?"

"Of course. Is it likely that I should wish to wear it on my bare breast after it has been rubbing against your soiled armour?"

Without another word I unhooked the necklace and handed it to her. She ran to a little distance, and, with one of those swift movements that were common to her, fastened it about her own neck. Then she returned, and threw the great strings of pearls, which she had removed to make place for it, over my head.

"Now have you found the woman of that dream, Olaf?" she asked, turning herself about in the moonlight.

I shook my head and answered:

"Nay, Augusta; but I fear that *you* have found misfortune. When it comes, I pray you to remember that you promised not to wear the necklace. Also that your soldier, Olaf, Thorvald's son, would have given his life rather than that you should have done so, not for the sake of any dream, but for your sake, Augusta, whom it is his business to protect."

"Would, then, it were your business either to protect me a little more, or a little less!" she exclaimed bitterly.

Having uttered this dark saying, she vanished from the terrace still wearing the string of golden shells.

On the following morning the necklace was returned to me by Irene's favourite lady, who smiled as she gave it to me. She was a dark-eyed, witty, and able girl named Martina, who had been my friend for a long while.

"The Augusta said that you were to examine this jewel to see that it has not been changed."

"I never suggested that the Augusta was a thief," I replied, "therefore it is unnecessary."

"She said also that I was to tell you, in case you should think that it has been befouled by her wearing of it, that she has had it carefully cleaned."

"That is thoughtful of her, Martina, for it needed washing. Now, will you take the Augusta's pearls, which she left with me in error?"

"I have no orders to take any pearls, Captain Olaf, although I did notice that two of the finest strings in the Empire are missing. Oh! you great northern child," she added in a whisper, "keep the pearls, they are a gift, and worth a prince's ransom; and take whatever else you can get, and keep that too."[*]

> [*] I have no further vision concerning these priceless
> pearls and do not know what became of them. Perhaps I
> was robbed of them during my imprisonment, or perhaps I
> gave them to Heliodore or to Martina. Where are they now,
> I wonder?—Editor.

Then, before I could answer her, she was gone.

For some weeks after this I saw no more of the Augusta, who appeared to avoid me. One day, however, I was summoned to her presence in her private apartments by the waiting-lady Martina, and went, to find her alone, save for Martina. The first thing that I noticed was that she wore about her neck an exact copy of the necklace of golden shells and emerald beetles; further, that about her waist was a girdle and on her wrist a bracelet of similar design. Pretending to see nothing, I saluted and stood to attention.

"Captain," she began, "yonder"—and she waved her hand towards the city, so that I could not fail to see the shell bracelet—"the uncles of my son, the Emperor, lie in prison. Have you heard of the matter, and, if so, what have you heard?"

"I have heard, Augusta, that the Emperor having been defeated by the Bulgarians, some of the legions proposed to set his uncle, Nicephorus—he who has been made a priest—upon the throne. I have heard further that thereon the Emperor caused the Cæsar Nicephorus to be blinded, and the tongues of the two other Cæsars and of their two brothers, the *Nobilissimi*, to be slit."

"Do you think well of such a deed, Olaf?"

"Augusta," I answered, "in this city I make it my business not to think, for if I did I should certainly go mad."

"Still, on this matter I command you to think, and to speak the truth of your thoughts. No harm shall come to you, whatever they may be."

"Augusta, I obey you. I think that whoever did this wicked thing must be a devil, either returned from that hell of which everyone is so fond of talking here, or on the road thither."

"Oh! you think that, do you? So I was right when I told Martina that there was only one honest opinion to be had in Constantinople and I knew where to get it. Well, most severe and indignant judge, suppose I tell you it was I who commanded that this deed should be done. Then would you change your judgment?"

"Not so, Augusta. I should only think much worse of you than ever I did before. If these great persons were traitors to the State, they should have been executed. But to torment them, to take away the sight of heaven and to bring them to the level of dumb beasts, all that their actual blood may not be on the tormentors' hand—why, the act is vile. So, at least, it would be held in those northern lands which you are pleased to call barbarian."

Now Irene sprang from her seat and clapped her hands for joy.

"You hear what he says, Martina, and the Emperor shall hear it too; aye, and so shall my ministers, Stauracius and Aetius, who supported him in this matter. I alone withstood him; I prayed him for his soul's sake to be merciful. He answered that he would no longer be governed by a woman; that he knew how to safeguard his empire, and what conscience should allow and what refuse. So, in spite of all my tears and prayers, the vile deed was done, as I think for no good cause. Well, it cannot be undone. Yet, Olaf, I fear that it may be added to, and that these royal-born men may be foully murdered. Therefore, I put you in charge of the prison where they lie. Here is the signed order. Take with you what men you may think needful, and hold that place, even should the Emperor himself command you to open. See also that the prisoners within are cared for and have all they need, but do not suffer them to escape."

I saluted and turned to go, when Irene called me back.

At that moment, too, in obedience to some sign which she made, Martina left the chamber, looking at me oddly as she did so. I came and stood before the Empress, who, I noted, seemed somewhat troubled, for her breast heaved and her gaze was fixed upon the floor now. It was of mosaic, and represented a heathen goddess talking to a young man, who stood before her with his arms folded. The goddess was angry with the man, and held in her left hand a dagger as though she would stab him, although her right arm was stretched out to embrace him and her attitude was one of pleading.

Irene lifted her head, and I saw that her fine eyes were filled with tears.

"Olaf," she said, "I am in much trouble, and I know not where to find a friend."

I smiled and answered:

"Need an Empress seek far for friends?"

"Aye, Olaf; farther than anyone who breathes. An Empress can find flatterers and partisans, but not a single friend. Such love her only for what she can give them. But, if fortune went against her, I say that they would fall away like leaves from a tree in a winter frost, so that she stood naked to every bitter blast of heaven. Yes, and then would come the foe and root up that tree and burn it to give them warmth and to celebrate their triumph. So I think, Olaf, it will be with me before all is done. Even my son hates me, Olaf, my only child for whose true welfare I strive night and day."

"I have heard as much, Augusta," I said.

"You have heard, like all the world. But what else of ill have you heard of me, Olaf? Speak out, man; I'm here to learn the truth."

"I have heard that you are very ambitious, Augusta, and that you hate your son as much as he hates you, because he is a rival to your power. It is rumoured that you would be glad if he were dead and you left to reign alone."

"Then a lie is rumoured, Olaf. Yet it is true that I am ambitious, who see far and would build this tottering empire up afresh. Olaf, it is a bitter thing to have begotten a fool."

"Then why do you not marry again and beget others, who might be no fools, Augusta?" I asked bluntly.

"Ah! why?" she answered, flashing a curious glance upon me. "In truth, I do not quite know why; but from no lack of suitors, since, were she but a hideous hag, an empress would find these. Olaf, you may have learned that I was not born in the purple. I was but a Greek girl of good race, not even noble, to whom God gave a gift of beauty; and when I was young I saw a man who took my fancy, also of old race, yet but a merchant of fruits which they grow in Greece and sell here and at Rome. I wished to marry him, but my mother, a far-seeing woman, said that such beauty as mine—though less than that of your Iduna the Fair, Olaf—was worth money or rank. So they sent away my merchant of fruits, who married the daughter of another merchant of fruits and throve very well in business. He came to see me some years ago, fat as a tub, his face scored all over with the marks of the spotted sickness, and we talked about old times. I gave him a concession to import dried fruits into Byzantium—that is what he came to see me for—and now he's dead. Well, my mother was right, for afterwards this poor beauty of mine took the fancy of the late Emperor, and, being very pious, he married me. So the Greek girl, by the will of God, became Augusta and the first woman in the world."

"By the will of God?" I repeated.

"Aye, I suppose so, or else all is raw chance. At least, I, who to-day might have been bargaining over dried fruits, as I should have done had I won my will, am—what you know. Look at this robe," and she spread her glittering dress before me. "Hark to the tramp of those guards before my door. Why, you are their captain. Go into the antechambers, and see the ambassadors waiting there in the hope of a word with the Ruler of the Earth! Look at my legions mustered on the drilling-grounds, and understand how great the Grecian girl has grown by virtue of the face which is less beauteous than that of—Iduna the Fair!"

"I understand all this, Augusta," I answered. "Yet it would seem that you are not happy. Did you not tell me just now that you could not find a friend and that you had begotten a fool?"

"Happy, Olaf? Why, I am wretched, so wretched that often I think the hell of which the priests preach is here on earth, and that I dwell in its hottest fires. Unless love hides it, what happiness is there in this life of ours, which must end in blackest death?"

"Love has its miseries also, Augusta. That I know, for once I loved."

"Aye, but then the love was not true, for this is the greatest curse of all—to love and not to be beloved. For the sake of a perfect love, if it could be won—why, I'd sacrifice even my ambition."

"Then you must keep your ambition, Augusta, since in this world you'll find nothing perfect."

"Olaf, I'm not so sure. Thoughts have come to me. Olaf, I told you that I have no friend in all this glittering Court. Will you be my friend?"

"I am your honest servant, Augusta, and I think that such a one is the best of friends."

"That's so; and yet no man can be true friend to a woman unless he is—more than friend. Nature has writ it so."

"I do not understand," I answered.

"You mean that you will not understand, and perhaps you are wise. Why do you stare at that pavement? There's a story written on it. The old goddess of my people, Aphrodite, loved a certain Adonis—so runs the fable—but he loved not her, and thought only of his sports. Look, she woos him there, and he rejects her, and in her rage she stabs him."

"Not so," I answered. "Of the end of the story I know nothing, but, if she had meant to kill him, the dagger would be in her right hand, not in her left."

"That's true, Olaf; and in the end it was Fate which killed him, not the goddess whom he had scorned. And yet, Olaf, it is not wise to scorn goddesses. Oh! of what do I talk? You'll befriend me, will you not?"

"Aye, Augusta, to the last drop of my blood, as is my duty. Do I not take your pay?"

"Then thus I seal our friendship and here's an earnest of the pay," Irene said slowly, and, bending forward, she kissed me on the lips.

At this moment the doors of the chamber were thrown open. Through them, preceded by heralds, that at once drew back again, entered the great minister Stauracius, a fat, oily-faced man with a cunning eye, who announced in a high, thin voice,

"The ambassadors of the Persians wait upon you, Augusta, as you appointed at this hour."

CHAPTER II
THE BLIND CÆSAR

Irene turned upon the eunuch as a she-lion turns upon some hunter that disturbs it from its prey. Noting the anger in her eyes, he fell back and prostrated himself. Thereupon she spoke to me as though his entry had interrupted her words.

"Those are the orders, Captain Olaf. See that you forget none of them. Even if this proud eunuch, who dares to appear before me unannounced, bids you to do so, I shall hold you to account. To-day I leave the city for a while for the Baths whither I am sent. You must not accompany me because of the duty I have laid upon you here. When I return, be sure I'll summon you," and, knowing that Stauracius could not see her from where he lay, for a moment she let her splendid eyes meet my own. In them there was a message I could not mistake.

"The Augusta shall be obeyed," I answered, saluting. "May the Augusta return in health and glory and more beautiful than— —"

"Iduna the Fair!" she broke in. "Captain, you are dismissed."

Again I saluted, retreating from the presence backwards and staying to bow at each third step, as was the custom. The process was somewhat long, and as I reached the door I heard her say to Stauracius,

"Hearken, you dog. If ever you dare to break in upon me thus again, you shall lose two things—your office and your head. What! May I not give secret orders to my trusted officer and not be spied upon by you? Now, cease your grovellings and lead in these Persians, as you have been bribed to do."

Passing through the silk-clad, bejewelled Persians who waited in an antechamber with their slaves and gifts, I gained the great terrace of the palace which looked upon the sea. Here I found Martina leaning on the parapet.

"Have you more of the Augusta's pearls about you, Olaf?" she asked mockingly, speaking over her shoulder.

"Not I, Martina," I answered, halting beside her.

"Indeed. I could have sworn otherwise, for they are perfumed, and I seemed to catch their odour. When did you begin to use the royal scent upon that yellow beard of yours, Olaf? If any of us women did so, it would mean blows and exile; but perchance a captain of the guard may be forgiven."

"I use no scents, girl, as you know well. Yet it is true that these rooms reek of them, and they cling to armour."

"Yes, and still more to hair. Well, what gift had my mistress for you to-day?"

"A commission to guard certain prisoners, Martina."

"Ah! Have you read it yet? When you do, I think you'll find that it names you Governor of the jail, which is a high office, carrying much pay and place. You are in good favour, Olaf, and I hope that when you come to greatness you will not forget Martina. It was I who put it into a certain mind to give you this commission as the only man that could be trusted in the Court."

"I do not forget a friend, Martina," I answered.

"That is your reputation, Olaf. Oh! what a road is opening to your feet. Yet I doubt you'll not walk it, being too honest; or, if you do, that it will lead you—not to glory, but a grave."

"Mayhap, Martina, and to speak truth, a grave is the only quiet place in Constantinople. Mayhap, too, it hides the only real glory."

"That's what we Christians say. It would be strange if you, who are not a Christian, alone should believe and keep the saying. Oh!" She went on with passion, "we are but shams and liars, whom God must hate. Well, I go to make ready for this journey to the Baths."

"How long do you stay there?" I asked.

"The course of waters takes a month. Less than that time does not serve to clear the Augusta's skin and restore her shape to the lines of youth which it begins to need, though doubtless you do not think so. You were named to come as her officer of the Person; but, Olaf, this other business rose up of a new governor for the jail in which the Cæsars and *Nobilissimi* are confined. I saw a chance for you in it, who, although you have served all these years, have had no real advancement, and mentioned your name, at which the Augusta leapt. To tell the truth, Olaf, I was not sure that you would wish to be captain of the guard at the Baths. Was I right or was I wrong?"

"I think you were right, Martina. Baths are idle places where folk drift into trouble, and I follow duty. Martina—may I say it to you?—you are a good woman and a kind. I pray that those gods of yours whom you worship may bless you."

"You pray in vain, Olaf, for that they will never do. Indeed, I think that they have cursed me."

Then suddenly she burst into tears, and, turning, went away.

I, too, went away somewhat bewildered, for much had happened to me that morning which I found it hard to understand. Why had the Augusta kissed me? I took it that this was some kind of imperial jest. It was known that I kept aloof from women, and she may have desired to see what I should do when an Augusta kissed me, and then to make a mock of me. I had heard that she had done as much with others.

Well, let that be, since Stauracius, who always feared lest a new favourite should slip between him and power, had settled the matter for me, for which I blessed Stauracius, although at the moment, being but a man, I had cursed him. And now why did Martina—the little, dark Martina with the kind face and the watchful, beady eyes, like to those of a robin in our northern lands—speak as she had done, and then burst into tears?

A doubt struck me, but I, who was never vain, pushed it aside. I did not understand, and of what use was it to try to interpret the meaning of the moods of women? My business was war, or, at the moment, the service that has to do with war, not women. Wars had brought me to the rank I held, though, strangely enough, of those wars I can recall nothing now; they have vanished from my vision. To wars also I looked to advance me in the future, who was no courtier, but a soldier, whom circumstances had brought to Court. Well, thanks to Martina, as she said, or to some caprice of the Empress, I had a new commission that was of more worth to me than her random kisses, and I would go to read it.

Read it I did in the little private room upon the palace wall which was mine as captain of the Augusta's guard, though, being written in Greek, I found this difficult. Martina had spoken truly. I was made the Governor of the State prison, with all authority, including that of life and death should emergency arise. Moreover, this governorship gave me the rank of a general, with a general's pay, also such pickings as I chose to take. In short, from captain of the guard, suddenly I had become a great man in Constantinople, one with whom even Stauracius and others like him would have to reckon, especially as his signature appeared upon the commission beneath that of the Empress.

Whilst I was wondering what I should do next, a trumpet blew upon the ramparts, and a Northman of my company entered, saluted and said that I was summoned. I went out, and there before me stood a dazzling band that bowed humbly to me, whom yesterday they would have passed without notice. Their captain, a smooth-faced Greek, came forward, and, addressing me as "General," said the imperial orders were that he was to escort me to the State jail.

"For what purpose?" I asked, since it came to my mind that Irene might have changed her fancy and issued another kind of commission.

"As its General and Governor, Illustrious," he replied.

"Then I will lead," I answered, "do you follow behind me."

Thus that vision ends.

In the next I see myself dwelling in some stately apartments that formed the antechambers to the great prison. This prison, which was situated not far from the Forum of Constantine, covered a large area of ground, which included a garden where the prisoners were allowed to walk. It was surrounded by a double wall, with an outer and an inner moat, the outer dry, and the inner filled with water. There were double gates also, and by them guard-towers. Moreover, I see a little yard, with posts in it, where prisoners were scourged, and a small and horrible room, furnished with a kind of wooden bed, to which they were bound for the punishment of the putting out of their eyes and the slitting of their tongues. In front of this room was a block where those condemned to death were sometimes executed.

There were many prisoners, not common felons, but people who had been taken for reasons of State or sometimes of religion. Perhaps in all they numbered a hundred men, and with them a few women, who had a quarter to themselves. Besides the jailers, three-score guards were stationed there night and day, and of all of these I was in command.

Before I had held my office three days I found that Irene had appointed me to it with good reason. It happened thus. The most of the prisoners were allowed to receive presents of food and other things sent to them by their friends. All these presents were supposed to be inspected by the officer in charge of the prison. This rule, which had been much neglected, I enforced again, with the result that I made some strange discoveries.

Thus, on the third day, there came a magnificent offering of figs for the Cæsars and *Nobilissimi*, the brothers-in-law of Irene and the uncles of the young Emperor Constantine, her son. These figs were being carried past me formally, when something about the appearance of one of them excited my suspicion. I took it and offered it to the jailer who carried the basket. He looked frightened, shook his head, and said,

"General, I touch no fruit."

"Indeed," I answered. "That is strange, since I thought that I saw you eating of it yesterday."

"Aye, General," he replied; "the truth is that I ate too much."

Making no answer, I went to the window, and threw the fig to a long-tailed, tame monkey which was chained to a post in the yard without. It caught it and ate greedily.

"Do not go away, friend," I said to the jailer, who was trying to depart while my back was turned. "I have questions that I would ask you."

So I spoke to him about other matters, and all the while watched the monkey.

Soon I saw that it was ill at ease. It began to tear at its stomach and to whimper like a child. Then it foamed at the mouth, was seized with convulsions, and within a quarter of an hour by the water-clock was dead.

"It would seem that those figs are poisoned, friend," I said, "and therefore it is fortunate for you that you ate too much fruit yesterday. Now, man, what do you know of this matter?"

"Nothing, sir," he answered, falling on his knees. "I swear to you by Christ, nothing. Only I doubted. The fruits were brought by a woman whom I thought that once I had seen in the household of the Augustus Constantine, and I knew — —" and he paused.

"Well, what did you know, man? It would be best to tell me quickly, who have power here."

"I knew, sir, what all the world knows, that Constantine would be rid of his uncles, whom he fears, though they are maimed. No more, I swear it, no more."

"Perhaps before the Augusta returns you may remember something more," I said. "Therefore, I will not judge your case at present. Ho! guard, come hither."

As he heard the soldiers stirring without in answer to my summons, the man, who was unarmed, looked about his desperately; then he sprang at the fruit, and, seizing a fig, strove to thrust it into his mouth. But I was too quick for him, and within a few seconds the soldiers had him fast.

"Shut this man in a safe dungeon," I said. "Treat and feed him well, but search him. See also that he does himself no harm and that none speak with him. Then forget all this business."

"What charge must be entered in the book, General?" asked the officer, saluting.

"A charge of stealing figs that belonged to the Cæsar Nicephorus and his royal brethren," I answered, and looked through the window.

He followed my glance, saw the poor monkey lying dead, and started.

"All shall be done," he said, and the man was led away.

When he had gone, I sent for the physician of the jail, whom I knew to be trustworthy, since I had appointed him myself. Without telling him anything, I bade him examine and preserve the figs, and also dissect the body of the monkey to discover why it died.

He bowed and went away with the fruit. A while later he returned, and showed me an open fig. In the heart of it was a pinch of white powder.

"What is it?" I asked.

"The deadliest poison that is known, General. See, the stalk has been drawn out, the powder blown in through a straw, and then the stalk replaced."

"Ah!" I said, "that is clever, but not quite clever enough. They have mixed the stalks. I noted that the purple fig had the stalk of a green fig, and that is why I tried it on the monkey."

"You observe well, General."

"Yes, Physician, I observe. I learned that when, as a lad, I hunted game in the far North. Also I learned to keep silent, since noise frightens game. Do you as much."

"Have no fear," he answered; and went about his business with the dead monkey.

When he had gone I thought a while. Then I rose, and went to the chapel of the prison, or, rather, to a place whence I could see those in the chapel without being seen. This chapel was situated in a gloomy crypt, lighted only with oil lamps that hung from the massive pillars and arches. The day was the Sabbath of the Christians, and when I entered the little secret hollow in the walls, the sacrament was being administered to certain of the prisoners.

Truly it was a sad sight, for the ministering priest was none other than the Cæsar Nicephorus, the eldest of the Emperor's uncles, who had been first ordained in order that he might be unfit to sit upon the throne, and afterwards blinded, as I have told. He was a tall, pale man, with an uncertain mouth and a little pointed chin, apparently between forty and fifty years of age, and his face was made dreadful by two red hollows where the eyes should have been. Yet, notwithstanding this disfigurement, and his tonsured crown, and the broidered priest's robes which hung upon him awkwardly, as he stumbled through the words of his office, to this poor victim there still seemed to cling some air of royal birth and bearing. Being blind, he could not see to administer the Element, and therefore his hand was guided by one of his imperial brethren, who also had been made a priest. The tongue of this priest had been slit, but now and again he gibbered some direction into the ear of Nicephorus. By the altar, watching all, sat a stern-faced monk, the confessor of the Cæsars and of the *Nobilissimi*, who was put there to spy upon them.

I followed the rite to its end, observing these unhappy prisoners seeking from the mystery of their faith the only consolation that remained to them. Many of them were men innocent of any crime, save that of adherence to some fallen cause, political or religious; victims were they, not sinners, to be released by death alone. I remember that, as the meaning of the scene came home to me, I recalled the words of Irene, who had said that she believed this world to be a hell, and found weight in them. At length, able to bear no more, I left my hiding-place and went into the garden behind the chapel. Here, at least, were natural things. Here flowers, tended by the prisoners, bloomed as they might have done in some less accursed spot. Here the free birds sang and nested in the trees, for what to them were the high surrounding walls?

I sat myself down upon a seat in the shade. Presently, as I had expected, Nicephorus, the priest-Cæsar, and his four brethren came into the garden. Two of them led the blind man by the hand, and the other two clung close to him, for all these unfortunates loved each other dearly. The four with the split tongues gabbled in his ears. Now and again, when he could catch or guess at the meaning of a word, he answered the speaker gently; or the others, seeing that he had not understood them aright, painfully tried to explain the error. Oh! it was a piteous thing to see and hear. My gorge rose against the young brute of an Emperor and his councillors who, for ambition's sake, had wrought this horrible crime. Little did I know then that ere long their fate would be his own, and that a mother's hand would deal it out to him.

They caught sight of me seated beneath the tree, and chattered like startled starlings, till at length Nicephorus understood.

"What say you, dear brothers?" he asked, "that the new governor of the prison is seated yonder? Well, why should we fear him? He has been here but a little while, yet he has shown himself very kind to us. Moreover, he is a man of the North, no treacherous Greek, and the men of the North are brave and upright. Once, when I was a free prince, I had some of them in my service, and I loved them well. Our nephew, the Emperor, offered a large sum to a Northman to blind or murder me, but he would not do it, and was dismissed from the service of the Empire because he spoke his mind and prayed his heathen gods to bring a like fate upon Constantine himself. Lead me to this governor; I would talk with him."

So they brought Nicephorus to me, though doubtfully, and when he was near I rose from my seat and saluted him. Thereon they all gabbled again with their split tongues, till at length he understood and flushed with pleasure.

"General Olaf," he said to me, "I thank you for your courtesy to a poor prisoner, forgotten by God and cruelly oppressed by man. General Olaf, the promise is of little worth, but, if ever it should be in my power, I will remember this kindness, which pleases me more than did the shouting of the legions in the short day of my prosperity."

"Sir," I answered, "whatever happens I shall remember your words, which are more to me than any honours kings can bestow. Now, sir, I will ask your royal brethren to fall back, as I wish to speak with you."

Nicephorus made a sign with his hand, and the four half-dumb men, all of whom resembled him strangely, especially in the weakness of their mouths and chins, obeyed. Bowing to me in a stately fashion, they withdrew, leaving us alone.

"Sir," I said, "I would warn you that you have enemies whom you may not suspect, for my duty here wherewith I was charged by the Augusta is not to oppress but to protect you and your imperial brothers."

Then I told him the story of the poisoned figs.

When he had heard it, the tears welled from his hollow eyes and ran down his pale cheeks.

"Constantine, my brother Leo's son, has done this," he said, "for never will he rest until all of us are in the grave."

"He is cruel because he fears you, O Nicephorus, and it is said that your ambition has given him cause to fear."

"Once, General, that was true," the prince replied. "Once, foolishly, I did aspire to rule; but it is long ago. Now they have made a priest of me, and I seek peace only. Can I and my brethren help it if, mutilated though we are, some still wish to use us against the Emperor? I tell you that Irene herself is at the back of them. She would set us on high that afterwards she may throw us down and crush us."

"I am her servant, Prince, and may not listen to such talk, who know only that she seeks to protect you from your enemies, and for that reason has placed me here, it seems not in vain. If you would continue to live, I warn you and your brethren to fly from plots and to be careful of what you eat and drink."

"I do not desire to live, General," he answered. "Oh! that I might die. Would that I might die."

"Death is not difficult to find, Prince," I replied, and left him.

These may seem hard words, but, be it remembered, I was no Christian then, but a heathen man. To see one who had been great and fallen from his greatness, one whom Fortune had deserted utterly, whining at Fate like a fretful child, and yet afraid to seek his freedom, moved me to contempt as well as to pity. Therefore, I spoke the words.

Yet all the rest of that day they weighed upon my mind, for I knew well how I should have interpreted them were I in this poor Cæsar's place. So heavily did they weigh that, during the following night, an impulse drew me from my bed and caused me to visit the cells in which these princes were imprisoned. Four of them were dark and silent, but in that of Nicephorus burned a light. I listened at the door, and through the key-place heard that the prisoner within was praying, and sobbing as he prayed.

Then I went away; but when I reached the end of the long passage something drew me back again. It was as though a hand I could not see were guiding me. I returned to the door of the cell, and now through it heard choking sounds. Quickly I shot the bolts and unlocked it with my master-key. This was what I saw within:

To a bar of the window-place was fastened such a rope as monks wear for a girdle; at the end of the rope was a noose, and in that noose the head of Nicephorus. There he hung, struggling. His hands had gripped the rope above his head, for though he had sought Death, at the last he tried to escape him. Of such stuff was Nicephorus made. Yet it was too late, or would have been, for as I entered the place his hands slipped from the thin cord, which tightened round his throat, choking him.

My sword was at my side. Drawing it, with a blow I cut the rope and caught him in my arms. Already he was swooning, but I poured water over his face, and, as his neck remained unbroken, he recovered his breath and senses.

"What play is this, Prince?" I asked.

"One that you taught me, General," he answered painfully. "You said that death could be found. I went to seek him, but at the last I feared. Oh! I tell you that when I thrust away that stool, my blind eyes were opened, and I saw the fires of hell and the hands of devils grasping at my soul to plunge it into them. Blessings be on you who have saved me from those fires," and seizing my hand he kissed it.

"Do not thank me," I said, "but thank the God you worship, for I think that He must have put it into my mind to visit you to-night. Now swear to me by that God that you will attempt such a deed no more, for if you will not swear then you must be fettered."

Then he swore so fervently by his Christ that I was sure he would never break the oath. After he had sworn I told him how I could not rest because of the strange fears which oppressed me.

"Oh!" he said, "without doubt it was God who sent His angel to you that I might be saved from the most dreadful of all sins. Without doubt it was God, Who knows you, although you do not know Him."

After this he fell upon his knees, and, having untied the cut rope from the window bars, I left him.

Now I tell this story because it has to do with my own, for it was these words of the Prince that first turned me to the study of the Christian Faith. Indeed, had they never been spoken, I believe that I should have lived and died a heathen man. Hitherto I had judged of that Faith by the works of those who practised it in Constantinople, and found it wanting. Now, however, I was sure that some Power from above us had guided me to the chamber of Nicephorus in time to save his life, me, who, had he died, in a sense would have been guilty of his blood. For had he not been driven to the deed by my bitter, mocking words? It may be said that this would have mattered little; that he might as well have died by his own hand as be taken to Athens, there to perish with his brethren, whether naturally or by murder

I do not know. But who can judge of such secret things? Without doubt the sufferings of Nicephorus had a purpose, as have all our sufferings. He was kept alive for reasons known to his Maker though not to man.

Here I will add that of this unhappy Cæsar and his brethren I remember little more. Dimly I seem to recollect that during my period of office some attack was made upon the prison by those who would have put the prince to death, but that I discovered the plot through the jailer who had introduced the poisoned figs, and defeated it with ease, thereby gaining much credit with Irene and her ministers. If so, of this plot history says nothing. All it tells of these princes is that afterwards a mob haled them to the Cathedral of St. Sophia and there proclaimed Nicephorus emperor. But they were taken again, and at last shipped to Athens, where they vanished from the sight of men.

God rest their tortured souls, for they were more sinned against than sinning.

CHAPTER III
MOTHER AND SON

The next vision of this Byzantine life of mine that rises before me is that of a great round building crowned with men clad in bishops' robes. At least they wore mitres, and each of them had a crooked pastoral staff which in most cases was carried by an attendant monk.

Some debate was in progress, or rather raging. Its subject seemed to be as to whether images should or should not be worshipped in churches. It was a furious thing, that debate. One party to it were called Iconoclasts, that was the party which did not like images, and I think the other party were called Orthodox, but of this I am not sure. So furious was it that I, the general and governor of the prison, had been commanded by those in authority to attend in order to prevent violence. The beginnings of what happened I do not remember. What I do remember is that the anti-Iconoclasts, the party to which the Empress Irene belonged, that was therefore the fashionable sect, being, as it seemed to me, worsted in argument, fell back on violence.

There followed a great tumult, in which the spectators took part, and the strange sight was seen of priests and their partisans, and even of bishops themselves, falling upon their adversaries and beating them with whatever weapon was to hand; yes, even with their pastoral staves. It was a wonderful thing to behold, these ministers of the Christ of peace belabouring each other with pastoral staves!

The party that advocated the worship of images was the more numerous and had the greater number of adherents, and therefore those who thought otherwise were defeated. A few of them were dragged out into the street and killed by the mob which waited there, and more were wounded, notwithstanding all that I and the guards could do to protect them. Among the Iconoclasts was a gentle-faced old man with a long beard, one of the bishops from Egypt, who was named Barnabas. He had said little in the debate, which lasted for several days, and when he spoke his words were full of charity and kindness. Still, the image faction hated him, and when the final tumult began some of them set upon him. Indeed, one brawny, dark-faced bishop—I think it was he of Antioch—rushed at Barnabas, and before

I could thrust him back, broke a jewelled staff upon his head, while other priests tore his robe from neck to shoulder and spat in his face.

At last the riot was quelled; the dead were borne away, and orders came to me that I was to convey Barnabas to the State prison if he still lived, together with some others, of whom I remember nothing. So thither I took Barnabas, and there, with the help of the prison physician—he to whom I had given the poisoned figs and the dead monkey to be examined—I nursed him back to life and health.

His illness was long, for one of the blows which he had received crippled him, and during it we talked much together. He was a very sweet-natured man and holy, a native of Britain, whose father or grandfather had been a Dane, and therefore there was a tie between us. In his youth he was a soldier. Having been taken prisoner in some war, he came to Italy, where he was ordained a priest at Rome. Afterwards he was sent as a missionary to Egypt, where he was appointed the head of a monastery, and in the end elected to a bishopric. But he had never forgotten the Danish tongue, which his parents taught him as a child, and so we were able to talk together in that language.

Now it would seem that since that night when the Cæsar Nicephorus strove to hang himself, I had obtained and studied a copy of the Christian Scriptures—how I do not know—and therefore was able to discuss these matters with Barnabas the bishop. Of our arguments I remember nothing, save that I pointed out to him that whereas the tree seemed to me to be very good, its fruits were vile beyond imagination, and I instanced the horrible tumult when he had been wounded almost to death, not by common men, but by the very leaders of the Christians.

He answered that these things must happen; that Christ Himself had said He came to bring not peace but a sword, and that only through war and struggle would the last truth be reached. The spirit was always good, he added, but the flesh was always vile. These deeds were those of the flesh, which passed away, but the spirit remained pure and immortal.

The end of it was that under the teaching of the holy Barnabas, saint and martyr (for afterwards he was murdered by the followers of the false prophet, Mahomet), I became a Christian and a new man. Now at length I understood what grace it was that had given me courage to offer battle to the heathen god, Odin, and to smite him down. Now I saw also where shone the light which I had been seeking these many years. Aye, and I clasped that light to my bosom to be my lamp in life and death.

So a day came when my beloved master, Barnabas, who would allow no delay in this matter, baptised me in his cell with water taken from his drinking vessel, charging me to make public profession before the Church when opportunity should arise.

It was just at this time that Irene returned from the Baths, and I sent to her a written report of all that had happened at the prison since I had been appointed its governor. Also I prayed that if it were her will I might be relieved of my office, as it was one which did not please me.

A few days later, while I sat in my chamber at the prison writing a paper concerning a prisoner who had died, the porter at the gate announced that a messenger from the Augusta wished to see me. I bade him show in the messenger, and presently there entered no chamberlain or eunuch, but a woman wrapped in a dark cloak. When the man had gone and the door was shut, she threw off the cloak and I saw that my visitor was Martina, the favourite waiting-lady of the Empress. We greeted each other warmly, who were always friends, and I asked her tidings.

"My tidings are, Olaf, that the waters have suited the Augusta very well. She has lost several pounds in weight and her skin is now like that of a young child."

"All health to the Augusta!" I said, laughing. "But you have not come here to tell me of the state of the royal skin. What next, Martina?"

"This, Olaf. The Empress has read your report with her own eyes, which is a rare thing for her to do. She said she wished to see whether or no you could write Greek. She is much pleased with the report, and told Stauracius in my presence that she had done well in choosing you for your office while she was absent from the city, since thereby she had saved the lives of the Cæsars and *Nobilissimi*, desiring as she does that these princes should be kept alive, at any rate for the present. She accedes also to your prayer, and will relieve you of your office as soon as a new governor can be chosen. You are to return to guard her person, but with your rank of general confirmed."

"That is all good news, Martina; so good that I wonder what sting is hidden in all this honey."

"That you will find out presently, Olaf. One I can warn you of, however—the sting of jealousy. Advancement such as yours draws eyes to you, not all of them in love."

I nodded and she went on:

"Meantime your star seems to shine very bright indeed. One might almost say that the Augusta worshipped it, at least she talks of you to me continually, and once or twice was in half a mind to send for you to the

Baths. Indeed, had it not been for reasons of State connected with your prisoners I think she would have done so."

"Ah!" I said, "now I think I begin to feel another sting in the honey."

"Another sting in the honey! Nay, nay, you mean a divine perfume, an essence of added sweetness, a flavour of the flowers on Mount Ida. Why, Olaf, if I were your enemy, as I dare say I shall be some day, for often we learn to hate those whom we have—rather liked, your head and your shoulders might bid good-bye to each other for such words as those."

"Perhaps, Martina; and if they did I do not know that it would greatly matter—now."

"Not greatly matter, when you are driving at full gallop along Fortune's road to Fame's temple with an Empress for your charioteer! Are you blind or mad, Olaf, or both? And what do you mean by your 'now'? Olaf, something has happened to you since last we met. Have you fallen in love with some fair prisoner in this hateful place and been repulsed? Such a fool as you are might take refusal even from a captive in his own hands. At least you are different."

"Yes, Martina, something has happened to me. I have become a Christian."

"Oh! Olaf, now I see that you are not a fool, as I thought, but very clever. Why, only yesterday the Augusta said to me—it was after she had read that report of yours—that if you were but a Christian she would be minded to lift you high indeed. But as you remained the most obstinate of heathens she did not see how it could be done without causing great trouble."

"Now I wish one could be a Christian within and remain a pagan without," I answered grimly; "though alas! that may not be. Martina, do you not understand that it was for no such reasons as these that I kissed the Cross; that in so doing I sought not fortune, but to be its servant?"

"By the Saints! you'll be tonsured next, and ill enough it would suit you," she exclaimed. "Remember, if things grow too—difficult, you can always be tonsured, Olaf. Only then you will have to give up the hope of that lady who wears the other half of the necklace somewhere. I don't mean Irene's sham half, but the real one. Oh! stop blushing and stammering, I know the story, and all about Iduna the Fair also. An exalted person told it me, and so did you, although you were not aware that you had done so, for you are not one who can keep a secret to himself. May all the guardian angels help that necklace-lady if ever she should meet another lady whom I will not name. And now why do you talk so much? Are you learning to preach, or what? If you really do mean to become a monk, Olaf, there is another thing you must give up, and that is war, except of the kind which you saw at the Council the other day. God above us! what a sight it would be to see you battering another bishop with a hook-shaped staff over a question of images or the Two Natures. I should be sorry for that bishop. But you haven't told me who converted you."

"Barnabas of Egypt," I said.

"Oh! I hoped that it had been a lady saint; the story would have been so much more interesting to the Court. Well, our imperial mistress does not like Barnabas, because he does not like images, and that may be a sting in *her* honey. But perhaps she will forgive him for your sake. You'll have to worship images."

"What do I care about images? It is the spirit that I seek, Martina, and all these things are nothing."

"You are thorough, as usual, Olaf, and jump farther than you can see. Well, be advised and say naught for or against images. As they have no meaning for you, what can it matter if they are or are not there? Leave them to the blind eyes and little minds. And now I must be gone, who can listen to your gossip no longer. Oh! I had forgotten my message. The Augusta commands that you shall wait on her this evening immediately after she has supped. Hear and obey!"

Having delivered this formal mandate, to neglect which meant imprisonment, or worse, she threw her cloak about her, and with a wondering glance at my face, opened the door and went.

At the hour appointed, or, rather, somewhat before it, I attended at the private apartments of the palace. Evidently I was expected, for one of the chamberlains, on seeing me, bowed and bade me be seated, then left the ante-room. Presently the door opened again, and through it came Martina, clad in her white official robe.

"You are early, Olaf," she said, "like a lover who keeps a tryst. Well, it is always wise to meet good fortune half way. But why do you come clad in full armour? It is not the custom to wait thus upon the Empress at this hour when you are off duty."

"I thought that I was on duty, Martina."

"Then, as usual, you thought wrong. Take off that armour; she says that the sight of it always makes her feel cold after supper. I say take it off; or if you cannot, I will help you."

So the mail was removed, leaving me clad in my plain blue tunic and hose.

"Would you have me come before the Empress thus?" I asked.

By way of answer she clapped her hands and bade the eunuch who answered the signal to bring a certain robe. He went, and presently reappeared with a wondrous garment of silk broidered with gold, such as nobles of high rank wore at festivals. This robe, which fitted as though it had been made for me, I put on, though I liked the look of it little. Martina would have had me even remove my sword, but I refused, saying:

"Except at the express order of the Empress, I and my sword are not parted."

"Well, she said nothing about the sword, Olaf, so let it be. All she said was that I must be careful that the robe matched the colour of the necklace you wear. She cannot bear colours which jar upon each other, especially by lamp-light."

"Am I a man," I asked angrily, "or a beast being decked for sacrifice?"

"Fie, Olaf, have you not yet forgotten your heathen talk? Remember, I pray you, that you are now a Christian in a Christian land."

"I thank you for reminding me of it," I replied; and that moment a chamberlain, entering hurriedly, commanded my presence.

"Good luck to you, Olaf," said Martina as I followed him. "Be sure to tell me the news later—or to-morrow."

Then the chamberlain led me, not into the audience hall, as I had expected, but to the private imperial dining chamber. Here, reclining upon couches in the old Roman fashion, one on either side of a narrow table on which stood fruits and flagons of rich-hued Greek wine, were the two greatest people in the world, the Augusta Irene and the Augustus Constantine, her son.

She was wonderfully apparelled in a low-cut garment of white silk, over which fell a mantle of the imperial purple, and I noted that on her dazzling bosom hung that necklace of emerald beetles separated by golden shells which she had caused to be copied from my own. On her fair hair that grew low upon her forehead and was parted in the middle, she wore a diadem of gold in which were set emeralds to match the beetles of the necklace. The Augustus was arrayed in the festal garments of a Cæsar, also covered with a purple cloak. He was a heavy-faced and somewhat stupid-looking youth, dark-haired, like his father and uncles, but having large, blue, and not unkindly eyes. From his flushed face I gathered that he had drunk well of the strong Greek wine, and from the sullen look about his mouth that, as was common, he had been quarrelling with his mother.

I stood at the end of the table and saluted first the Empress and then the Emperor.

"Who's this?" he asked, glancing at me.

"General Olaf, of my guard," she answered, "Governor of the State Prison. You remember, you wished me to send for him to settle the point as to which we were arguing."

"Oh! yes. Well, General Olaf, of my mother's guard, have you not been told that you should salute the Augustus before the Augusta?"

"Sire," I answered humbly, "I have heard nothing of that matter, but in the land where I was bred I was taught that if a man and a woman were together I must always bow first to the woman and then to the man."

"Well said," exclaimed the Empress, clapping her hands; but the Emperor answered: "Doubtless your mother taught you that, not your father. Next time you enter the imperial chamber be pleased to forget the lesson and to remember that Emperors and Empresses are not men and women."

"Sire," I answered, "as you command I will remember that Emperors and Empresses are not men and women, but Emperors and Empresses."

At these words the Augustus began to scowl, but, changing his mind, laughed, as did his mother. He filled a gold cup with wine and pushed it towards me, saying:

"Drink to us, soldier, for after you have done so, our wits may be better matched."

I took the cup and holding it, said:

"I pledge your Imperial Majesties, who shine upon the world like twin stars in the sky. All hail to your Majesties!" and I drank, but not too deep.

"You are clever," growled the Augustus. "Well, keep the cup; you've earned it. Yet drain it first, man. You have scarce wet your lips. Do you fear that it is poisoned, as you say yonder fruits are?" And he pointed to a side-table, where stood a jar of glass in which were those very figs that had been sent to the princes in the prison.

"The cup you give is mine," interrupted Irene; "still, my servant is welcome to the gift. It shall be sent to your quarters, General."

"A soldier has no need of such gauds, your Majesties," I began, when Constantine, who, while we spoke, had swallowed another draught of the strong wine, broke in angrily:

"May I not give a cup of gold but you must claim it, I to whom the Empire and all its wealth belong?"

Snatching up the beaker he dashed it to the floor, spilling the wine, of which I, who wished to keep my head cool, was glad.

"Have done," he went on in his drunken rage. "Shall the Cæsars huckster over a piece of worked gold like Jews in a market? Give me those figs, man; I'll settle the matter of this poison."

I brought the jar of figs, and, bowing, set them down before him. That they were the same I knew, for the glass was labelled in my own writing and in that of the physician. He cut away the sealed parchment which was stretched over the mouth of the jar.

"Now hearken you, Olaf," he said. "It is true that I ordered fruit to be sent to that fool-Cæsar, my uncle, because the last time I saw him Nicephorus prayed me for it, and I was willing to do him a pleasure. But that I ordered the fruit to be poisoned, as my mother says, is a lie, and may God curse the tongue that spoke it. I will show you that it was a lie," and plunging his hand into the spirit in the jar, he drew out two of the figs. "Now," he went on, waving them about in a half-drunken fashion, "this General Olaf of yours says that these are the same figs which were sent to the Cæsar, I mean the blind priest, Father Nicephorus. Don't you, Olaf?"

"Yes, Sire," I answered, "they were placed in that bottle in my presence and sealed with my seal."

"Well, those figs were sent by me, and this Olaf tells us they are poisoned. I'll show him, and you too, mother, that they are *not* poisoned, for I will eat one of them."

Now I looked at the Augusta, but she sat silent, her arms folded on her white bosom, her handsome face turned as it were to stone.

Constantine lifted the fig towards his loose mouth. Again I looked at the Augusta. Still she sat there like a statue, and it came into my mind that it was her purpose to allow this wine-bemused man to eat the fig. Then I acted.

"Augustus," I said, "you must not touch that fruit," and stepping forward I took it from his hand.

He sprang to his feet and began to revile me.

"You watch-dog of the North!" he shouted. "Do you dare to say to the Emperor that he shall not do this or that? By all the images my mother worships I'll have you whipped through the Circus."

"That you will never do," I answered, for my free blood boiled at the insult. "I tell you, Sire," I went on, leaving out certain words which I meant to speak, "that the fig is poisoned."

"And I tell you that you lie, you heathen savage. See here! Either you eat that fig or I do, so that we may know who speaks the truth. If you won't, I will. Now obey, or, by Christ! to-morrow you shall be shorter by a head."

"The Augustus is pleased to threaten, which is unnecessary," I remarked. "If I eat the fig, will the Augustus swear to leave the rest of them uneaten?"

"Aye," he answered with a hiccough, "for then I shall know the truth, and for the truth I live, though," he added, "I haven't found it yet."

"And if I do not eat it, will the Augustus do so?"

"By the Holy Blood, yes. I'll eat a dozen of them. Am I one to be hectored by a woman and a barbarian? Eat, or I eat."

"Good, Sire. It is better that a barbarian should die than that the world should lose its glorious Emperor. I eat, and when you are as I soon shall be, as will happen even to an emperor, may my blood lie heavy on your soul, the blood which I give to save your life."

Then I lifted the fig to my lips.

Before ever it touched them, with a motion swift as that of a panther springing on its prey, Irene had leapt from her couch and dashed the fruit from my hand. She turned upon her son.

"What kind of a thing are you," she asked, "who would suffer a brave man to poison himself that he may save your worthless life? Oh! God, what have I done that I should have given birth to such a hound? Whoever poisoned them, these fruits are poisoned, as has been proved and can be proved again, yes, and shall be. I tell you that if Olaf had tasted one of them by now he would have been dead or dying."

Constantine drank another cup of wine, which, oddly enough, seemed to sober him for the moment.

"I find all this strange," he said heavily. "You, my mother, would have suffered me to eat the fig which you declare is poisoned; a matter whereof you may know something. But when the General Olaf offers to eat it in my place, with your own royal hand you dash it from his lips, as he dashed it from mine. And there is another thing which is still more strange. This Olaf, who also says the figs are poisoned, offered to eat one of them if I promised I would not do so, which means, if he is right, that he offered to give his life for mine. Yet I have done nothing for him except call him hard names; and as he is your servant he has nothing to look for from me if I should win the fight with you at last. Now I have heard much talk of miracles, but this is the only one I have ever seen. Either Olaf is a liar, or he is a great man and a saint. He says, I am told, that the monkey which ate one of those figs died. Well, I never thought of it before, but there are more monkeys in the palace. Indeed, one lives on the terrace near by, for I fed it this afternoon. We'll put the matter to the proof and learn of what stuff this Olaf is really made."

On the table stood a silver bell, and as he spoke he struck it. A chamberlain entered and was ordered to bring in the monkey. He departed, and with incredible swiftness the beast and its keeper arrived. It was a large animal of the baboon tribe, famous throughout the palace for its tricks. Indeed, on entering, at a word from the man who led it, it bowed to all of us.

"Give your beast these," said the Emperor, handing the keeper several of the figs.

The baboon took the fruits and, having sniffed at them, put them aside. Then the keeper fed it with some sweetmeats, which it caught and devoured, and presently, when its fears were allayed, threw it one of the figs, which it swallowed, doubtless thinking it a sweetmeat. A minute or two later it began to show signs of distress and shortly afterwards died in convulsions.

"Now," said Irene, "now do you believe, my son?"

"Yes," he answered, "I believe that there is a saint in Constantinople. Sir Saint, I salute you. You have saved my life and if it should come my way, by your brother saints! I'll save yours, although you are my mother's servant."

So speaking, he drank off yet another cup of wine and reeled from the room.

The keeper, at a sign from Irene, lifted up the body of the dead ape and also left the chamber, weeping as he went, for he had loved this beast.

CHAPTER IV
OLAF OFFERS HIS SWORD

The Emperor had gone, drunk; the ape had gone, dead; and its keeper had gone, weeping. Irene and I alone were left in that beautiful place with the wine-stained table on which stood the jar of poisoned figs and the bent golden cup lying on the marble floor.

She sat upon the couch, looking at me with a kind of amazement in her eyes, and I stood before her at attention, as does a soldier on duty.

"I wonder why he did not send for one of my servants to eat those figs—Stauracius, for instance," she mused, adding with a little laugh, "Well, if he had, there are some whom I could have spared better than that poor ape, which at times I used to feed. It was an honest creature, that ape; the only creature in the palace that would not rub its head in the dust before the Augusta. Ah! now I remember, it always hated Constantine, for when he was a child he used to tease it with a stick, getting beyond the length of its chain and striking it. But one day, as he passed too near, it caught him and buffeted him on the cheek and tore out some of his hair. He wanted to kill it then, but I forbade him. Yet he has never forgotten it, he who never does forget anything he hates, and that is why he sent for the poor beast."

"The Augusta will remember that the Augustus did not know that the figs were poisoned."

"The Augusta is sure that the Augustus knew well enough that those figs were poisoned, at any rate from the moment that I dashed one of them from your lips, Olaf. Well, I have made a bitterer enemy than before, that's all. They say that by Nature's rule mother and child must love each other, but it is a lie. I tell you it's a lie. From the time he was tiny I hated that boy, though not half as much as he has hated me. You are thinking to yourself that this is because our ambitions clash like meeting swords, and that from them spring these fires of hate. It is not so. The hate is native to our hearts, and will only end when one of us lies dead at the other's hand."

"Terrible words, Augusta."

"Yes, but true. Truth is always terrible—in Byzantium. Olaf, take those drugged fruits and set them in the drawer of yonder table; lock it and guard the key, lest they should poison other honest animals."

I obeyed and returned to my station.

She looked at me and said:

"I grow weary of the sight of you standing there like a statue of the Roman Mars, with your sword half hid beneath your cloak; and, what's more, I hate this hall; it reeks of Constantine and his drink and lies. Oh! he's vile, and for my sins God has made me his mother, unless, indeed, he was changed at birth, as I've been told, though I could never prove it. Give me your hand and help me to rise. So, I thank you. Now follow me. We'll sit a while in my private chamber, where alone I can be happy, since the Emperor never comes there. Nay, talk not of duty; you have no guards to set or change to-night. Follow me; I have secret business of which I would talk with you."

So she went and I followed through doors that opened mysteriously at our approach and shut mysteriously behind us, till I found myself in a little room half-lighted only, that I had never seen before. It was a scented and a beautiful place, in one corner of which a white statue gleamed, that of a Venus kissing Cupid, who folded one wing about her head, and through the open window-place the moonlight shone and floated the murmur of the sea.

The double doors were shut, for aught I knew locked, and with her own hands Irene drew the curtains over them. Near the open window, to which there was no balcony, stood a couch.

"Sit yonder, Olaf," she said, "for here there is no ceremony; here we are but man and woman."

I obeyed, while she busied herself with the curtains. Then she came and sat herself down on the couch also, leaning against the end of it in such a fashion that she could watch me in the moonlight.

"Olaf," she said, after she had looked at me a while, rather strangely, as I thought, for the colour came and went upon her face, which in that light seemed quite young again and wonderfully beautiful, "Olaf, you are a very brave man."

"There are hundreds in your service braver, Empress; cowards do not take to soldiering."

"I could tell you a different story, Olaf; but it was not of this kind of courage that I talked. It was of that which made you offer to eat the poisoned fig in place of Constantine. Why did you do so? It is true that, as things have happened, he'll remember it in your favour, for I'll say this of him, he never forgets one who has saved him from harm, any more than he forgets one who has harmed him. But if you had eaten you would have died, and then how could he have rewarded you?"

"Empress, when I took my oath of office I swore to protect both the Augustus and the Augusta, even with my life. I was fulfilling my oath, that is all."

"You are a strange man as well as a brave man to interpret oaths so strictly. If you will do as much as this for one who is nothing to you, and who has never paid you a gold piece, how much, I wonder, would you do for one whom you love."

"I could offer no more than my life for such a one, Empress, could I?"

"Someone told me—it may have been you, Olaf, or another—that once you did more, challenging a heathen god for the sake of one you loved, and defeating him. It was added that this was for a man, but that I do not believe. Doubtless it was for the sake of Iduna the Fair, of whom you have spoken to me, whom it seems you cannot forget although she was faithless to you. It is said that the best way to hold love is to be faithless to him who loves, and in truth I believe it," she added bitterly.

"You are mistaken, Empress. It was to be avenged on him for the life of Steinar, my foster-brother, which he had taken in sacrifice, that I dared Odin and hewed his holy statue to pieces with this sword; of Steinar, whom Iduna betrayed as she betrayed me, bringing one to death and the other to shame."

"At least, had it not been for this Iduna you would never have given battle to the great god of the North and thus brought his curse upon you. For, Olaf, those gods live; they are devils."

"Whether Odin is or is not, I do not fear his curse, Empress."

"Yet it will find you out before all is done, or so I think. Look you, pagan blood still runs in me, and, Christian though I am, I would not dare one of the great gods of Greece and Rome. I'd leave that to the priests. Do you fear nothing, Olaf?"

"I think nothing at all, since I hewed off Odin's head and came away unscathed."

"Then you are a man to my liking, Olaf."

She paused, looking at me even more strangely than before, till I turned my eyes, indeed, and stared out at the sea, wishing that I were in it, or anywhere away from this lovely and imperious woman whom I was sworn to obey in all things.

"Olaf," she said presently, "you have served me well of late. Is there any reward that you would ask, and if so, what? Anything that I can give is yours, unless," she added hastily, "the gift will take you away from Constantinople and from—me."

"Yes, Augusta," I answered, still staring out at the sea. "In the prison yonder is an old bishop named Barnabas of Egypt, who was set upon by other bishops at the Council while you were away and wellnigh beaten to death. I ask that he may be freed and restored to his diocese with honour."

"Barnabas," she replied sharply. "I know the man. He is an Iconoclast, and therefore my enemy. Only this morning I signed an order that he should be kept in confinement till he died, here or elsewhere. Still," she went on, "though I would sooner give you a province, have your gift, for I can refuse you nothing. Barnabas shall be freed and restored to his see with honour. I have said."

Now I began to thank her, but she stopped me, saying:

"Have done! Another time you can talk to me of heretics with whom you have made friends, but I, who hear enough of such, would have no more of them to-night."

So I grew silent and still stared out at the sea. Indeed, I was wondering in my mind whether I dared ask leave to depart, for I felt her eyes burning on me, and grew much afraid. Suddenly I heard a sound, a gentle sound of rustling silk, and in another instant I felt Irene's arms clasped about me and Irene's head laid upon my knee. Yes, she was kneeling before me, sobbing, and her proud head was resting on my knee. The diadem she wore had fallen from it, and her tresses, breaking loose, flowed to the ground, and lay there gleaming like gold in the moonlight.

She looked up, and her face was that of a weeping saint.

"Dost understand?" she whispered.

Now despair took me, which I knew full well would soon be followed by madness. Then came a thought.

"Yes," I said hoarsely. "I understand that you grieve over that matter of the Augustus and the poisoned figs, and would pray me to keep silence. Have no fear, my lips are sealed, but for his I cannot answer, though perhaps as he had drunk so much——"

"Fool!" she whispered. "Is it thus that an Empress pleads with her captain to keep silence?" Then she drew herself up, a wonderful look upon her face that had grown suddenly white, a fire in her upturned eyes, and for the second time kissed me upon the lips.

I took her in my arms and kissed her back. For an instant my mind swam. Then in my soul I cried for help, and strength came to me. Rising, I lifted her as though she were a child, and stood her on her feet. I said:

"Hearken, Empress, before destruction falls. I do understand now, though a moment ago I did not, who never thought it possible that the queen of the world could look with favour upon one so humble."

"Love takes no account of rank," she murmured, "and that kiss of yours upon my lips is more to me than the empire of the world."

"Yet hearken," I answered. "There is another wall between us which may not be climbed."

"Man, what is this wall? Is it named woman? Are you sworn to the memory of that Iduna, who is more fair than I? Or is it, perchance, her of the necklace?"

"Neither. Iduna is dead to me; she of the necklace is but a dream. The wall is that of your own faith. On this night seven days ago I was baptised a Christian."

"Well, what of it? This draws us nearer."

"Study the sayings of your sacred book, Empress, and you will find that it thrusts us apart."

Now she coloured to her hair, and a kind of madness took her.

"Am I to be preached to by you?" she asked.

"I preach to myself, Augusta, who need it greatly, not to you, who mayhap do not need it."

"Hating me as you do, why should you need it? You are the worst of hypocrites, who would veil your hate under a priest's robe."

"Have you no pity, Irene? When did I say that I hated you? Moreover, if I had hated you, should I— —" and I ceased.

"I do not know what you would or would not have done," she answered coldly. "I think that Constantine is right, and that you must be what is called a saint; and, if so, saints are best in heaven, especially when they know too much on earth. Give me that sword of yours."

I drew the sword, saluted with it, and gave it to her.

"It is a heavy weapon," she said. "Whence came it?"

"From the same grave as the necklace, Augusta."

"Ah! the necklace that your dream-woman wore. Well, go to seek her in the land of dreams," and she lifted the sword.

"Your pardon, Augusta, but you are about to strike with the blunt edge, which may wound but will not kill."

She laughed a little, very nervously, and, turning the sword round in her hand, said:

"Truly, you are the strangest of men! Ah! I thank you, now I have it right. Do you understand, Olaf, I mean, Sir Saint, what sort of a story I must tell of you after I have struck? Do you understand that not only are you about to die, but that infamy will be poured upon your name and that your body will be dragged through the streets and thrown to the dogs with the city offal? Answer, I say, answer!"

"I understand that you must cause these things to be done for your own sake, Augusta, and I do not complain. Lies matter nothing to me, who journey to the Land of Truth, where there are some whom I would meet again. Be advised by me. Strike here, where the neck joins the shoulder, holding the sword slantwise, for there even a woman's blow will serve to sever the great artery."

"I cannot. Kill yourself, Olaf."

"A week ago I'd have fallen on the sword; but now, by the rule of our faith, in such a cause I may not. My blood must be upon your hands, for which I grieve, knowing that no other road is open to you. Augusta, if it is worth anything to you, take my full forgiveness for the deed, and with it my thanks for all the goodness you have shown to me, but most for your woman's favour. In after years, perhaps, when death draws near to you also, if ever you remember Olaf, your faithful servant, you will understand much it is not fitting that I should say. Give me one moment to make my peace with Heaven as to certain kisses. Then strike hard and swiftly, and, as you strike, scream for your guards and women. Your wit will do the rest."

She lifted the sword, while, after a moment's prayer, I bared my neck of the silk robe. Then she let it fall again, gasping, and said:

"Tell me first, for I am curious. Are you no man? Or have you forsworn woman, as do the monks?"

"Not I, Augusta. Had I lived, some day I might have married, who would have wished to leave children behind me, since in our law marriage is allowed. Forget not your promise as to the Bishop Barnabas, who, I fear, will weep over this seeming fall of mine."

"So you would marry, would you?" she said, as one who speaks to herself; then thought awhile, and handed me back the sword.

"Olaf," she went on, "you have made me feel as I never felt before—ashamed, utterly ashamed, and though I learn to hate you, as it well may hap I shall, know that I shall always honour you."

Then she sank down upon the couch, and, hiding her face in her hands, wept bitterly.

It was at this moment that I went very near to loving Irene.

I think she must have felt something of what was passing in my mind, for suddenly she looked up and said: "Give me that jewel," and she pointed to the diadem on the floor, "and help me to order my hair; my hands shake."

"Nay," I said, as I gave her the crown. "Of that wine I drink no more. I dare not touch you; you grow too dear."

"For those words," she whispered, "go in safety, and remember that from Irene you have naught to fear, as I know well I have naught to fear from you, O Prince among men."

So presently I went.

On the following morning, as I sat in my office at the prison, setting all things in order for whoever should succeed me, Martina entered, as she had done before.

"How came you here unannounced?" I asked, when she was seated.

"By virtue of this," she answered, holding up her hand and showing on it a ring I knew. It was the signet of the Empress. I saluted the seal, saying:

"And for what purpose, Martina? To order me to bonds or death?"

"To bonds or death!" she exclaimed innocently. "What can our good Olaf have done worthy of such woes? Nay, I come to free one from bonds, and perhaps from death, namely, a certain heretic bishop who is named Barnabas. Here is the order for his release, signed by the Augusta's hand and sealed with her seal, under which he is at liberty to bide in Constantinople while he will and to return to his bishopric in Egypt when it pleases him. Also, if he holds that any have harmed him, he may make complaint, and it shall be considered without delay."

I took the parchment, read it, and laid it on the table, saying:

"The commands of the Empress shall be done. Is there aught else, Martina?"

"Yes. To-morrow morning you will be relieved of your office, and another governor—Stauracius and Aetius are quarrelling as to his name—will take your place."

"And I?"

"You will resume your post as captain of the private guard, only with the rank of a full general of the army. But that I told you yesterday. It is now confirmed."

I said nothing, but a groan I could not choke broke from my lips.

"You do not seem as pleased as you might be, Olaf. Tell me, now, at what hour did you leave the palace last night? While waiting for my mistress to summon me I fell asleep in the vestibule of the ante-room, and when I awoke and went into that room I found there the gold-broidered silk robe you wore, cast upon the ground, and your armour gone."

"I know not what was the hour, Martina, and speak no more to me, I pray, of that accursed womanish robe."

"Which you treated but ill, Olaf, for it is spotted as though with blood."

"The Augustus spilt some wine over it."

"Aye, my mistress told me the story. Also that of how you would have eaten the poisoned fig, which you snatched from the lips of Constantine."

"And what else did your mistress tell you, Martina?"

"Not much, Olaf. She was in a very strange mood last night, and while I combed her hair, which, Olaf, was as tangled as though a man had handled it," and she looked at me till I coloured to the eyes, "and undid her diadem, that was set on it all awry, she spoke to me of marriage."

"Of marriage!" I gasped.

"Certainly—did I not speak the word with clearness?—of marriage."

"With whom, Martina?"

"Oh! grow not jealous before there is need, Olaf. She made no mention of the name of our future divine master, for whosoever can rule Irene, if such a one lives, will certainly rule us also. All she said was that she wished she could find some man to guide, guard and comfort her, who grew lonely amidst many troubles, and hoped for more sons than Constantine."

"What sort of a man, Martina? This Emperor Charlemagne, or some other king?"

"No. She vowed that she had seen enough of princes, who were murderers and liars, all of them; and that what she desired was one of good birth, no more, brave, honest, and not a fool. I asked her, too, what she would have him like to look upon."

"And what did she say to that, Martina?"

"Oh! she said that he must be tall, and under forty, fair-haired and bearded, since she loved not these shaven effeminates, who look half woman and half priest; one who had known war, and yet was no ruffler; a person of open mind, who had learnt and could learn more. Well, now that I think of it, by all the Saints!—yes, much such a man as *you* are, Olaf."

"Then she may find them in plenty," I said, with an uneasy laugh.

"Do you think so? Well, she did not, neither did I. Indeed, she pointed out that this was her trouble. Among the great of the earth she knew no such man, and, if she sought lower, then would come jealousies and war."

"Indeed they would. Doubtless you showed her that this was so, Martina."

"Not at all, Olaf. I asked her of what use it was to be an Empress if she could not please her own heart in this matter of a husband, which is one important to a woman. I said also, as for such fears, that a secret marriage might be thought of, which is an honest business that could be declared when occasion came."

"And what did she answer to that, Martina?"

"She fell into high good humour, called me a faithful and a clever friend, gave me a handsome jewel, told me that she would have a mission for me on the morrow—doubtless that which I now fulfil, for I have heard of no other—said, notwithstanding all the trouble as to the Augustus and his threats, that she was sure she would sleep better than she had done for nights, kissed me on both cheeks, and flung herself upon her knees at her praying-stool, where I left her. But why are you looking so sad, Olaf?"

"Oh! I know not, save that I find life difficult, and full of pitfalls which it is hard to escape."

Martina rested her elbows on the table and her chin upon her little hand, staring me full in the face with her quick eyes that pierced like nails.

"Olaf," she said, "your star shines bright above you. Keep your eyes fixed thereon and follow it, and never think about the pitfalls. It may lead you I know not where."

"To heaven, perhaps," I suggested.

"Well, you did not fear to go thither when you would have eaten the poisoned fig last night. To heaven, perchance, but by a royal road. Whatever you may think of some others, marriage is an honourable estate, my Christian friend, especially if a man marries well. And now good-bye; we shall meet again at the palace, whither you will repair to-morrow morning. Not before, since I am engaged in directing the furnishment of your new quarters in the right wing, and, though the workmen labour all night, they will not be finished until then. Good-bye, General Olaf. Your servant Martina salutes you and your star," and she curtsied before me until her knees almost touched the ground.

CHAPTER V
AVE POST SECULA

It comes back to me that on the following day my successor in the governorship of the jail, who he was I know not now, arrived, and that to him in due form I handed over my offices and duties. Before I did so, however, I made it my care to release Barnabas, I think on the previous evening. In his cell I read the Augusta's warrant to the old bishop.

"How was it obtained, son," he asked, "for, know, that having so many enemies on this small matter of image worship, I expected to die in this place? Now it seems that I am free, and may even return to my charge in Egypt."

"The Empress granted it to me as a favour, Father," I answered. "I told her that you were from the North, like myself."

He studied me with his shrewd blue eyes, and said:

"It seems strange to me that so great and unusual a boon should be granted for such a reason, seeing that better men than I am have suffered banishment and worse woes for less cause than I have given. What did you pay the Empress for this favour, son Olaf?"

"Nothing, Father."

"Is it so? Olaf, a dream has come to me about you, and in that dream I saw you walk through a great fire and emerge unscathed, save for the singeing of your lips and hair."

"Perhaps they were singed, Father. Otherwise, I am unburned, though what will happen to me in the future I do not know, for my dangers seem great."

"In my dream you triumphed over all of them, Olaf, and also met with some reward even in this life, though now I know not what it was. Yes, and triumph you shall, my son in Christ. Fear nothing, even when the storm-clouds sweep about your head and the lightnings blind your eyes. I say, fear nothing, for you have friends whom you cannot see. I ask no more even under the seal of confession, since there are secrets which it is not well to learn. Who knows, I might go mad, or torture might draw from me words

I would not speak. Therefore, keep your own counsel, son, and confess to God alone."

"What will you do now, Father?" I asked. "Return to Egypt?"

"Nay, not yet awhile. It comes to me that I must bide here for a space, which under this pardon I have liberty to do, but to what end I cannot say. Later on I shall return, if God so wills. I go to dwell with good folk who are known to me, and from time to time will let you hear where I may be found, if you should need my help or counsel."

Then I led him to the gates, and, having given him a witnessed copy of his warrant of release, bade him farewell for that time, making it known to the guards and certain priests who lingered there that any who molested him must answer for it to the Augusta.

Thus we parted.

Having handed over the keys of the prison, I walked to the palace unattended, being minded to take up my duties there unnoticed. But this was not to be. As I entered the palace gate a sentry called out something, and a messenger, who seemed to be in waiting, departed at full speed. Then the sentry, saluting, told me that his orders were that I must stand awhile, he knew not why. Presently I discovered, for across the square within the gates marched a full general's guard, whereof the officer also saluted, and prayed me to come with him. I went, wondering if I was to be given in charge, and by him, surrounded with this pompous guard, was led to my new quarters, which were more splendid than I could have dreamed. Here the guard left me, and presently other officers appeared, some of them old comrades of my own, asking for orders, of which, of course, I had none to give. Also, within an hour, I was summoned to a council of generals to discuss some matter of a war in which the Empire was engaged. By such means as these it was conveyed to me that I had become a great man, or, at any rate, one in the way of growing great.

That afternoon, when, according to my old custom, I was making my round of the guards, I met the Augusta upon the main terrace, surrounded by a number of ministers and courtiers. I saluted and would have passed on, but she bade one of her eunuchs call me to her. So I came and stood before her.

"We greet you, General Olaf," she said. "Where have you been all this long while? Oh! I remember. At the State prison, as its governor, of which office you are now relieved at your own request. Well, the palace welcomes you again, for when you are here all within know themselves safe."

Thus she spoke, her great eyes searching my face the while, then bowed her head in token of dismissal. I saluted again, and began to step backwards, according to the rule, whereon she motioned to me to stand. Then she began to make a laugh of me to the painted throng about her.

"Say, nobles and ladies," she said, "did any of you ever see such a man? We address him as best we may—and we have reason to believe that he understands our language—yet not one word does he vouchsafe to us in answer. There he stands, like a soldier cut in iron who moves by springs, with never an 'I thank you' or a 'Good day' on his lips. Doubtless he would reprove us all, who, he holds, talk too much, being, as we all have heard, a man of stern morality, who has no tenderness for human foibles. By the way, General Olaf, a rumour has reached us that you have forsaken doubt, and become a Christian. Is this true?"

"It is true, Augusta."

"Then if as a Pagan you were a man of iron, what will you be as a Christian, we wonder? One hard as diamond, no less. Yet we are glad of this tidings, as all good servants of the Church must be, since henceforth our friendship will be closer and we value you. General, you must be received publicly into the bosom of the Faith; it will be an encouragement to others to follow your example. Perhaps, as you have served us so well in many wars and as an officer of our guard, we ourselves will be your god-mother. The matter shall be considered by us. What have you to answer to it?"

"Nothing," I replied, "save that when the Augusta has considered of the matter, I will consider of my answer."

At this the courtiers tittered, and, instead of growing angry, as I thought she might, Irene burst out laughing.

"Truly we were wrong," she said, "to provoke you to open your mouth, General, for when you do so, like that red sword you wear, your tongue is sharp, if somewhat heavy. Tell us, General, are your new quarters to your taste, and before you reply know that we inspected them ourselves, and, having a liking for such tasks, attended to their furnishment. 'Tis done, you will see, in the Northern style, which we think somewhat cold and heavy— like your sword and tongue."

"If the Augusta asks me," I said, "the quarters are too fine for a single soldier. The two rooms where I dwelt before were sufficient."

"A single soldier! Well, that is a fault which can be remedied. You should marry, General Olaf."

"When I find any woman who wishes to marry me and whom I wish to marry, I will obey the Augusta's commands."

"So be it, General, only remember that first we must approve the lady. Venture not, General, to share those new quarters of yours with any lady whom we do not approve."

Then, followed by the Court, she turned and walked away, and I went about my business, wondering what was the meaning of all this guarded and half-bitter talk.

The next event that returns to me clearly is that of my public acceptance as a Christian in the great Cathedral of St. Sophia, which must have taken place not very long after this meeting upon the terrace. I know that by every means in my power I had striven, though without avail, to escape this ceremony, pointing out that I could be publicly received into the body of the Church at any chapel where there was a priest and a congregation of a dozen humble folk. But this the Empress would not allow. The reason she gave was her desire that my conversion should be proclaimed throughout the city, that other Pagans, of whom there were thousands, might follow my example. Yet I think she had another which she did not avow. It was that I might be made known in public as a man of importance whom it pleased her to honour.

On the morning of this rite, Martina came to acquaint me with its details, and told me that the Empress would be present at the cathedral in state, making her progress thither in her golden chariot, drawn by the famed milk-white steeds. I, it seemed, was to ride after the chariot in my general's uniform, which was splendid enough, followed by a company of guards, and surrounded by chanting priests. The Patriarch himself, no less a person, was to receive me and some other converts, and the cathedral would be filled with all the great ones of Constantinople.

I asked whether Irene intended to be my god-mother, as she had threatened.

"Not so," replied Martina. "On that point she has changed her mind."

"So much the better," I said. "But why?"

"There is a canon of the Church, Olaf, which forbids intermarriage between a god-parent and his or her god-child," she replied dryly. "Whether this canon has come to the Augusta's memory or not, I cannot say. It may be so."

"Who, then, is to be my god-mother?" I asked hurriedly, leaving the problem of Irene's motives undiscussed.

"I am, by the written Imperial decree delivered to me not an hour ago."

"You, Martina, you who are younger than myself by many years?"

"Yes, I. The Augusta has just explained to me that as we seem to be such very good friends, and to talk together so much alone, doubtless, she supposed, upon matters of religion, there could be no person more suitable than such a good Christian as myself to fill that holy office."

"What do you mean, Martina?" I asked bluntly.

"I mean, Olaf," she replied, turning away her head, and speaking in a strained voice, "that, where you are concerned, the Augusta of late has done me the honour to be somewhat jealous of me. Well, of a god-mother no one need be jealous. The Augusta is a clever woman, Olaf."

"I do not quite understand," I said. "Why should the Augusta be jealous of you?"

"There is no reason at all, Olaf, except that, as it happens, she is jealous of every woman who comes near to you, and she knows that we are intimate and that you trust me—well, more, perhaps, than you trust her. Oh! I assure you that of late you have not spoken to any woman under fifty unnoted and unreported. Many eyes watch you, Olaf."

"Then they might find better employment. But tell me outright, Martina, what is the meaning of all this?"

"Surely even a wooden-headed Northman can guess, Olaf?"

She glanced round her to make sure that we were alone in the great apartment of my quarters and that the doors were shut, then went on, almost in a whisper, "My mistress is wondering whether or no she will marry again, and, if so, whether she will choose a certain somewhat over-virtuous Christian soldier as a second husband. As yet she has not made up her mind. Moreover, even if she had, nothing could be done at present or until the question of the struggle between her and her son for power is settled in this way or in that. Therefore, at worst, or at best, that soldier has yet a while of single life left to him, say a month or two."

"Then during that month or two perhaps he would be wise to travel," I suggested.

"Perhaps, if he were a fool who would run away from fortune, and if he could get leave of absence, which in his case is impossible; to attempt such a journey without it would mean his death. No, if he is wise, that soldier will bide where he is and await events, possessing his soul in patience, as a good Christian should do. Now, as your god-mother, I must instruct you in this service. Look not so troubled; it is really most simple. You know Stauracius, the eunuch, is to be your god-father, which is very fortunate for you, since, although he looks on you with doubt and jealousy, to blind or murder his own god-son would cause too much scandal even in Constantinople. As a special mark of grace, also, the Bishop Barnabas, of Egypt, will be allowed to assist in the ceremony, because it was he who snatched your soul from the burning. Moreover, since the Sacrament is to be administered afterwards, he has been commanded to attend here to receive your confession in the chapel of the palace, and within an hour. You know that this day being the Feast of St. Michael and All Angels, you will be received in the name of Michael, a high one well fitted to a warlike saint, though I think that I shall still call you Olaf. So farewell, my god-son to be, until we meet at the cathedral, where I shall shine in the reflected light of all your virtues."

Then she sighed, laughed a little, and glided away.

In due course a priest of the chapel came to summon me there, saying that the Bishop Barnabas awaited me. I went and made my confession, though in truth I had little to tell him that he did not already know. Afterwards the good old man, who by now was quite recovered from his hurts and imprisonment, accompanied me to my quarters, where we ate together. He told me that before he attended in the chapel he had been received by the Empress, who had spoken to him very kindly, making light of their difference of opinion as to images and with her own mouth confirmed him in his bishopric, even hinting at his possible promotion.

"This, my son," he added, "I am well aware I owe to your good offices."

I asked him if he would return at once to Upper Egypt, where he had his bishopric.

"No, my son," he answered, "not yet awhile. The truth is that there have arrived here the chief man in my diocese, and his daughter. He is a descendant of the old Pharaohs of the Egyptians who lives near the second cataract of the Nile, almost on the borders of Ethiopia, whither the accursed children of Mahomet have not yet forced their way. He is still a great man among the Egyptians, who look upon him as their lawful prince. His mission here is to try to plan a new war upon the followers of the Prophet, who, he holds, might be assailed by the Empire at the mouths of the Nile, while he attacked them with his Egyptians from the south."

Now I grew interested, who had always grieved over the loss of Egypt to the Empire, and asked what was this prince's name.

"Magas, my son, and his daughter is named Heliodore. Ah! she is such a woman as I would see you wed, beautiful indeed, and good and true as she is beautiful, with a high spirit also, such as befits her ancient blood.

Mayhap you will note her in the cathedral. Nay, I forgot, not there, but afterwards in this palace, since it is the command of the Empress, to whom I have been speaking of their matters, that these two should come to dwell here for a while. After that I hope we shall all return to Egypt together, though Magas, being on a secret mission, does not travel under his own name, but as a merchant."

Suddenly he paused, and began to stare at my throat.

"Is aught wrong with my armour, Father?" I asked.

"No, son. I was looking at that trinket which you wear. Of course I have noted it before, but never closely. It is strange, very strange!"

"What is strange, Father?"

"Only that I have seen another like it."

"I dare say you have," I answered, laughing, "for when I would not give this to the Augusta, it pleased her to have it copied."

"No, no; I mean in Egypt, and, what is more, a story hung to the jewel."

"On whom? Where? What story?" I asked eagerly.

"Oh! I cannot stay to tell you now. Moreover, your mind should be fixed upon immortal crowns, and not on earthly necklaces. I must be gone; nay, stay me not, I am already late. Do you get you to your knees and pray till your god-parents come to fetch you."

Then, in spite of all I could do to keep him, he went, muttering: "Strange! Exceeding strange!" and leaving me quite unfit for prayer.

An hour later I was riding through the streets of the mighty city, clad in shining armour. As the season was that of October, in which the Feast of St. Michael falls, we wore cloaks, although, the day being warm, they were little needed. Mine was of some fine white stuff, with a red cross broidered on the right shoulder. Stauracius, the eunuch and great minister, who had been ordered to act as my god-father, rode alongside of me on a mule, because he dared not mount a horse, sweating beneath his thick robe of office, and, as I heard from time to time, cursing me, his god-son, and all this ceremony beneath his breath. On my other hand was my god-mother, Martina, riding an Arab mare, which she did well enough, having been brought up to horsemanship on the plains of Greece. Her mood was varied, for now she laughed at the humour of the scene, and now she was sad almost to tears.

The streets were lined with thousands of the pleasure-loving people of the city, who had come out to see the show of the Empress going in state to the cathedral. They were gathered even on the flat house-tops and in the entrances to the public buildings and open places. But the glory of the sight was centred, not about me, with my escort of guards and chanting priests, but in Irene's self. Preceded and followed by glittering regiments of soldiers, she drove in her famous golden chariot, drawn by eight milk-white steeds, each of which was led by a bejewelled noble. Her dress was splendid and covered with sparkling gems, and on her yellow hair she wore a crown. As she went the multitudes shouted their welcome, and she bowed to right and left in answer to the shouts. Now and again, however, bands of armed men, clad in a dress of a peculiar colour, emerged from side streets and hooted, crying:

"Where is the Augustus? Give us the Augustus. We will not be ruled by a woman and her eunuchs!"

These men were of the party of Constantine, and set on by him. Once, indeed, there was a tumult, for some of them tried to bar the road, till they were driven away, leaving a few dead or wounded behind them. But still the crowds shouted and the Empress bowed as though nothing had happened, and thus by a somewhat winding route, we came to St. Sophia.

The Augusta entered, and presently I and those with me followed her into the wonderful cathedral. I see it now, not in particular, but as a whole, with its endless columns, its aisles and apses, and its glittering mosaics shining through the holy gloom, across which shot bars of light from the high window-places. All the great place was full of the noblest in the city, rank upon rank of them, come thither to see the Empress in her glory at the great Feast of St. Michael, which year by year she attended thus.

At the altar waited the Patriarch in his splendid robes, attended by many bishops and priests, among them Barnabas of Egypt. The service began, I and some other converts standing together near to the altar rail. The details of it do not return to me. Sweet voices sang, censers gave forth their incense, banners waved, and images of the saints, standing everywhere, smiled upon us fixedly. Some of us were baptised, and some who had already been baptised were received publicly into the fellowship of the Church, I among them. My god-father, Stauracius, a deacon prompting him, and my god-mother, Martina, spoke certain words on my behalf, and I also spoke certain words which I had learned.

The splendid Patriarch, a sour-faced man with a slight squint, gave me his especial blessing. The Bishop Barnabas, upon whom, as I noted, the Patriarch was always careful to turn his back, offered up a prayer. My god-father and god-mother embraced me, Stauracius smacking the air at a distance, for which I was grateful, and Martina touching me gently with her lips upon the brow. The Empress smiled upon me and, as I passed her, patted me on the shoulder. Then the Sacrament was celebrated, whereof the Empress partook first; next we converts, with our god-parents, and afterwards a number of the congregation.

It was over at last. The Augusta and her attendants marched down the cathedral towards the great western doors, priests followed, and, among them, we converts, whom the people applauded openly.

Looking to right and left of me, for I was weary of keeping my gaze fixed upon the floor, presently I caught sight of a face whilst as yet it was far away. It seemed to draw me, I knew not why. The face was that of a woman. She stood by an old and stately-looking man with a white beard, the last of a line of worshippers next to the aisle along which the procession passed, and I saw that she was young and fair.

Down the long, resounding aisle the procession marched slowly. Now I was nearer to the face, and perceived that it was lovely as some rich-hued flower. The large eyes were dark and soft as a deer's. The complexion, too, was somewhat dark, as though the sun had kissed it. The lips were red and curving, and about them played a little smile that was full of mystery as the eyes were full of thought and tenderness. The figure was delicate and rounded, but not so very tall. All these things and others I noted, yet it was not by them that I was drawn and held, but rather because I *knew this lady*.

She was the woman of whom, years ago, I had dreamed on the night on which I broke into the Wanderer's tomb at Aar!

Never for one moment did I doubt me of this truth. I was sure. I was sure. It did not even need, while she turned to whisper something to her companion, that the cloak she wore should open a little, revealing on her breast a necklace of emerald beetles separated by inlaid shells of pale and ancient gold.

She was watching the procession with interest, yet somewhat idly, when she caught sight of me, whom, from where she stood, she could scarcely have seen before. Of a sudden her face grew doubtful and troubled, like to that of one who has just received some hurt. She saw the ornament about my neck. She turned pale and had she not gripped the arm of the man beside her, would, I think, have fallen. Then her eyes caught mine, and Fate had us in its net.

She leaned forward, gazing, gazing, all her soul in those dark eyes, and I, too, gazed and gazed. The great cathedral vanished with its glittering crowds, the sound of chanting and of feet that marched died from my ears. In place of these I saw a mighty columned temple and two stone figures, taller than pines, seated on a plain, and through the moonlit silence heard a sweet voice murmuring:

"Farewell. For this life, farewell!"

Now we were near to each other, now I was passing her, I who might not stay. My hand brushed hers, and oh! it was as though I had drunk a cup of wine. A spirit entered into me and, bending, I whispered in her ear, speaking in the Latin tongue, since Greek, which all knew, I did not dare to use, "*Ave post secula!*" Greeting after the ages!

I saw her bosom heave; yes, and heard her whisper back:

"*Ave!*"

So she knew me also.

CHAPTER VI
HELIODORE

That night there was feasting at the palace, and I, Olaf, now known as Michael, as a convert was one of the chief guests, so that for me there was no escape. I sat very silent, so silent that the Augusta frowned, though she was too far off to speak to me. The banquet came to an end at last and before midnight I was free to go, still without word from the Empress, who withdrew herself, as I thought in an ill-humour.

I sought my bed, but in it knew little of sleep. I had found her for whom during all the long years I had been searching, though I did not understand that I was searching. After the ages I had found her and she had found me. Her eyes said it, and, unless I dreamed, her sweet voice said it also.

Who was she? Doubtless that Heliodore, daughter of Magas, the prince of whom the Bishop Barnabas had spoken to me. Oh! now I understood what he meant when he spoke of another necklace like to that I wore, and yet would explain nothing. It lay upon the breast of Heliodore, Heliodore who was such a one as he wished that I might wed. Well, certainly I wished it too; but, alas! how could I wed, who was in Irene's power, a toy for her to play with or to break? And how would it fare with any woman whom it was known that I wished to wed? I must be secret until she was gone from Constantinople, and in this way or in that I could follow her. I, who had ever been open-minded, must learn to keep my own counsel.

Now, too, I remembered how Barnabas had said the Augusta commanded that this Prince Magas and his daughter should come to the palace as her guests. Well, the place was vast, a town in itself, and likely enough I should not see them there. Yet I longed to see one of them as never I had longed for anything before. I was sure, also, that no fears could keep us apart, even though I knew the road before me to be full of dangers and of trials, knew that I went with my life in my hand, the life of which I had been quite careless, but that now had become so dear to me. For did not the world hold another to whom it belonged?

The night passed away. I rose and went about my morning duties. Scarcely were these finished when a messenger summoned me to the presence of the Augusta. I followed him with a sinking heart, certain that those woes which I had foreseen were about to begin. Also, now there was no woman in the whole world whom I less wished to see than Irene, Empress of the Earth.

I was led to the small audience chamber, whereof I have already spoken, that on the floor of which was the mosaic of the goddess Venus making pretence to kill her lover. There I found the Augusta seated in a chair of State, the minister Stauracius, my god-father, who glowered at me as I entered, some secretaries, and Martina, my god-mother, who was the lady in attendance.

I saluted the Empress, who bowed graciously and said:

"General Olaf—nay, I forgot, General Michael, your god-father Stauracius has something to say which I trust will please you as much as it does him and me. Speak, Stauracius."

"Beloved god-son," began Stauracius, in a voice of sullen rage, "it has pleased the Augusta to appoint you——"

"On the prayer and advice of me, Stauracius," interrupted the Empress.

"——On the prayer and advice of me, Stauracius," repeated the eunuch like a talking bird, "to be one of her chamberlains and Master of the Palace, at a salary of" (I forget the sum, but it was a great one) "with all the power and perquisites to that office pertaining, in reward of the services which you have rendered to her and the Empire. Thank the Empress for her gracious favour."

"Nay," interrupted Irene again, "thank your beloved god-father Stauracius, who has given me no peace until I offered you this preferment which has suddenly become vacant, Stauracius alone knows why, for I do not. Oh! you were wise, Olaf—I mean Michael—to choose Stauracius for a god-father, though I warn him," she added archly, "that in his natural love he must not push you forward too fast lest others should begin to show that jealousy which is a stranger to his noble nature. Come hither, Michael, and kiss my hand upon your appointment."

So I advanced and, kneeling, kissed the Augusta's hand, according to custom on such occasions, noting, as doubtless Stauracius did also, that she pressed it hard enough against my lips. Then I rose and said:

"I thank the Augusta——"

"And my god-father Stauracius," she interrupted.

"——And my god-father Stauracius," I echoed, "for her and his goodness towards me. Yet with humility I venture to say that I am a soldier who knows nothing whatsoever of the duties of a chamberlain and of a Master of the Palace, and, therefore, I beg that someone else more competent may be chosen to fill these high offices."

On hearing these words Stauracius stared at me with his round and owl-like eyes. Never before had he known an officer in Constantinople who wished to decline power and more pay. Scarcely, indeed, could he believe his ears. But the Augusta only laughed.

"Baptism has not changed you, Olaf," she said, "who ever were simple, as I believe your duties will be. At any rate, your god-father and god-mother will instruct you in them—especially your god-mother. So no more of such foolish talk. Stauracius, you may be gone to attend to the affairs of which we have been speaking, as I see you burn to do, and take those secretaries with you, for the scratching of their pens sets my teeth on edge. Bide here a moment, General, for as Master of the Palace it will be your duty to receive certain guests to-day of whom I wish to speak with you. Bide you also, Martina, that you may remember my words in case this unpractised officer should forget them."

Stauracius and his secretaries bowed themselves out, leaving the three of us alone.

"Now, Olaf, or Michael—which do you wish to be called?"

"It is more easy for a man to alter his nature than his name," I answered.

"Have you altered your nature? If so, your manners remain much what they were. Well, then, be Olaf in private and Michael in public, for often an alias is convenient enough. Hark! I would read you a lesson. As the wise King Solomon said, 'Everything has its place and time.' It is good to repent you of your sins and to think about your soul, but I pray you do so no more at my feasts, especially when they are given in your honour. Last night you sat at the board like a mummy at an Egyptian banquet. Had your skull stood on it, filled with wine, it could scarce have looked grimmer than did your face. Be more cheerful, I pray you, or I will have you tonsured and promoted to be a bishop, like that old heretic Barnabas of whom you are so fond. Ah! you smile at last, and I am glad to see it. Now hearken again. This afternoon there comes to the palace a certain old Egyptian named Magas, whom I place in your especial charge, and with him his wife—at least, I think she is his wife."

"Nay, Mistress, his daughter," interrupted Martina.

"Oh! his daughter," said the Augusta suspiciously. "I did not know she was his daughter. What is she like, Martina?"

"I have not seen her, Empress, but someone said that she is a black-looking woman, such as the Nile breeds."

"Is it so? Then I charge you, Olaf, keep her far from me, for I love not these ugly black women, whose woolly hair always smells of grease. Yes, I give you leave to court her, if you will, since thereby you may learn some secrets," and she laughed merrily.

I bowed, saying that I would obey the Augusta's orders to the best of my power, and she went on:

"Olaf, I would discover the truth concerning this Magas and his schemes, which as a soldier you are well fitted to find out. It seems he has a plan for the recovery of Egypt out of the hands of the followers of that accursed false prophet whose soul dwells with Satan. Now, I would win back Egypt, if I may, and thereby add glory to my name and the Empire. Hear all that he proposes, study it well, and make report to me. Afterwards I will see him alone, who for the present will send him a letter by the hand of Martina here bidding him open all his heart to you. For a week or more I shall have no time to spend upon this Magas, who must give myself to business upon which hangs my power and perchance my life."

These words she spoke heavily, then fell into a fit of brooding. Rousing herself, she went on:

"Did you note yesterday, Olaf, if you had any mind left for the things of earth, that as I drove in state through the streets many met me with sullen silence, while others cursed me openly and shouted, 'Where is the Augustus?' 'Give us Constantine. We will have no woman's rule.'"

"I saw and heard something of these things, Augusta; also that certain of the soldiers on guard in the city had a mutinous air."

"Aye, but what you did not see and hear was that a plot had been laid to murder me in the cathedral. I got wind of it in time and if you were still governor of yonder prison you'd know where the murderers are to-day. Yet they're but tools; it is their captains whom I want. Well, torture may make them speak; Stauracius has gone to see to it. Oh! the strife is fierce and doubtful. I walk blindfold along a precipice. Above are Fortune's heights, and beneath black ruin. Perhaps you'd be wise to get you to Constantine, Olaf, and become his man, as many are doing, since he'd be glad of you. No need to shake your head, for that's not your way; you are no hound to bite the hand that feeds you, like these street-bred dogs. Would that I could keep you nearer to me, where hour by hour you might help me with your counsel and your quiet strength. But it may not be—as yet. I raise you as high as I dare, but it must be done step by step, for even now some grow jealous.

Take heed to what you eat, Olaf. See that your guards are Northmen, and beneath your doublet wear mail, especially at night. Moreover, unless I send for you, do not come near me too often, and, when we meet, be my humble servant, like others; aye, learn to crawl and kiss the ground. Above all, keep secret as the grave.

"Now," she went on after a pause, during which I stood silent, "what is there more? Oh! with your new offices, you'll retain that of captain of my guard, for I would be well watched during these next few weeks. Follow up the matter of the Egyptian; you may find advancement in it. Perchance one day you will be the general I send against the Moslems—if I can spare you. On all this matter be secret also, for once rumour buzzes over it that peach rots. The Egyptian and his swarthy girl come to the palace to-day, when he will receive my letter. Meet him and see them well housed, though not too near me; Martina will help you. Now be gone and leave me to my battles."

So I went, and she watched me to the door with eyes that were full of tenderness.

Again there is a blank in my memory, or my vision. I suppose that Magas and his daughter Heliodore arrived at the palace on the day of my interview with Irene, of which I have told. I suppose that I welcomed them and conducted them to the guest house that had been made ready for them in the gardens. Doubtless, I listened eagerly to the first words which Heliodore spoke to me, save that one in the cathedral, the word of greeting. Doubtless, I asked her many things, and she gave me many answers. But of all this nothing remains.

What comes back to me is a picture of the Egyptian prince, Magas, and myself seated at some meal in a chamber overlooking the moonlit palace garden. We were alone, and this noble, white-bearded man, hook-nosed and hawk-eyed, was telling me of the troubles of his countrymen, the Christian Copts of Egypt.

"Look on me, sir," he said. "As I could prove to you, were it worth while, and as many could bear witness, for the records have been kept, I am a descendant in the true line from the ancient Pharaohs of my country. Moreover, my daughter, through her Grecian mother, is sprung from the Ptolemies. Our race is Christian, and has been for these three hundred years, although it was among the last to be converted. Yet, noble as we are, we suffer every wrong at the hands of the Moslems. Our goods and lands are doubly taxed, and, if we should go into the towns of Lower Egypt, we must wear garments on which the Cross is broidered as a badge of shame. Yet, where I live—near to the first cataract of the Nile, and not so very far from the city of old Thebes—the Prophet-worshippers have no real power. I am still the true ruler of that district, as the Bishop Barnabas will tell you, and at any moment, were my standard to be lifted, I could call three thousand Coptic spears to fight for Christ and Egypt. Moreover, if money were forthcoming, the hosts of Nubia could be raised, and together we might sweep down on the Moslems like the Nile in flood, and drive them back to Alexandria."

Then he went on to set out his plans, which in sum were that a Roman fleet and army should appear at the mouths of the Nile to besiege and capture Alexandria, and, with his help, massacre or drive out every Moslem in Egypt. The scheme, which he set forth with much detail, seemed feasible enough, and when I had mastered its particulars I promised to report it to the Empress, and afterwards to speak with him further.

I left the chamber, and presently stood in the garden. Although it was autumn time, the night in this mild climate was very warm and pleasant, and the moonlight threw black shadows of the trees across the paths. Under one of these trees, an ancient, green-leaved oak, the largest of a little grove, I saw a woman sitting. Perchance I knew who she was, perchance I had come thither to meet her, I cannot say. At least, this was not our first meeting by many, for as I came she rose, lifting her flower-like face towards my own, and next moment was in my arms.

When we had kissed our full, we began to talk, seated hand in hand beneath the oak.

"What have you been doing this day, beloved?" she asked.

"Much what I do every day, Heliodore. I have attended to my duties, which are threefold, as Chamberlain, as Master of the Palace, and as Captain of the Guard. Also, for a little while, I saw the Augusta, to whom I had to report various matters. The interview was brief, since a rumour had reached her that the Armenian regiments refuse to take the oath of fidelity to her alone, as she has commanded should be done, and demand that the name of the Emperor, her son, should be coupled with hers, as before. This report disturbed her much, so that she had little time for other business."

"Did you speak of my father's matter, Olaf?"

"Aye, shortly. She listened, and asked whether I were sure that I had got the truth from him. She added that I had best test it by what I could win from you by any arts that a man may use. For, Heliodore, because of something that my god-mother, Martina, said to her, it is fixed in her mind that you are black-skinned and very ugly. Therefore, the Augusta, who does not like any man about her to care for other women, thinks I may make love to you with safety. So I prayed for leave from my duties on the guard this evening that I might sup with your father in the guest-house, and see what I could learn from one or both of you."

"Love makes you clever, Olaf. But hearken. I do not believe that the Empress thinks me black and ugly any longer. As it chanced while I walked in the inner garden this afternoon, where you said I might go when I wished to be quite alone, dreaming of our love and you, I looked up and saw an imperial woman of middle age, who was gorgeous as a peacock, watching me from a little distance. I went on my way, pretending to see no one, and heard the lady say:

"'Has all this trouble driven me mad, Martina, or did I behold a woman beautiful as one of the nymphs of my people's fables wandering yonder among those bushes?'

"I repeat her very words, Olaf, not because they are true—for, remember, she saw me at a distance and against a background of rocks and autumn flowers—but because they were her words, which I think you ought to hear, with those that followed them."

"Irene has said many false things in her life," I said, smiling, "but by all the Saints these were not among them."

Then we embraced again, and after that was finished Heliodore, her head resting on my shoulder, continued her story:

"'What was she like, Mistress?' asked the lady Martina, for by this time I had passed behind some little trees. 'I have seen no one who is beautiful in this garden except yourself.'

"'She was clad in a clinging white robe, Martina, that left her arms and bosom bare'—being alone, Olaf, I wore my Egyptian dress beneath my cloak, which I had laid down because of the heat of the sun. 'She was not so very tall, yet rounded and most graceful. Her eyes seemed large and dark, Martina, like her hair; her face was tinted like a rich-hued rose. Oh! were I a man she seemed such a one as I should love, who, like all my people, have ever worshipped beauty. Yet, what did I say, that she put me in mind of a nymph of Greece. Nay, that was not so. It was of a goddess of Old Egypt that she put me in mind, for on her face was the dreaming smile which I have seen on that of a statue of mother Isis whom the Egyptians worshipped. Moreover, she wore just such a headdress as I have noted upon those statues.'

"Now the lady Martina answered: 'Surely, you must have dreamed, Mistress. The only Egyptian woman in the palace is the daughter of the old Coptic noble, Magas, who is in Olaf's charge, and though I am told that she is not so ugly as I heard at first, Olaf has never said to me that she was like a goddess. What you saw was doubtless some image of Fortune conjured up by your mind. This I take to be the best of omens, who in these doubtful days grow superstitious.'

"'Would Olaf tell one woman that another was like a goddess, Martina, even though she to whom he spoke was his god-mother and a dozen years younger than himself? Come,' she added, 'and let us see if we can find this Egyptian.'

"Then," Heliodore went on, "not knowing what to do, I stood still there against the rockwork and the flowers till presently, round the bushes, appeared the splendid lady and Martina."

Now when I, Olaf, heard all this, I groaned and said:

"Oh! Heliodore, it was the Augusta herself."

"Yes, it was the Augusta, as I learned presently. Well, they came, and I curtsied to them.

"'Are you the daughter of Magas, the Egyptian?' asked the lady, eyeing me from head to foot.

"'Yes, Madam,' I answered. 'I am Heliodore, the daughter of Magas. I pray that I have done no wrong in walking in this garden, but the General Olaf, the Master of the Palace, gave me leave to come here.'

"'And did the General Olaf, whom we know as Michael, give you that necklace which you wear, also, O Daughter of Magas? Nay, you must needs answer me, for I am the Augusta.'

"Now I curtsied again, and said:

"'Not so, O Augusta; the necklace is from Old Egypt, and was found upon the body of a royal lady in a tomb. I have worn it for many years.'

"'Indeed, and that which the General Michael wears came also from a tomb.'

"'Yes, he told me so, Augusta,' I said.

"'It would seem that the two must once have been one, Daughter of Magas?'

"'It may be so, Augusta; I do not know.'

"Now the Empress looked about her, and the lady Martina, dropping behind, began to fan herself.

"'Are you married, girl?' she asked.

"'No,' I answered.

"'Are you affianced?'

"Now I hesitated a little, then answered 'No' again.

"'You seem to be somewhat doubtful on the point. Farewell for this while. When you walk abroad in our garden, which is open to you, be pleased to array yourself in the dress of our country, and not in that of a courtesan of Egypt.'"

"What did you answer to that saying?" I asked.

"That which was not wise, I fear, Olaf, for my temper stirred me. I answered: 'Madam, I thank you for your permission to walk in your garden. If ever I should do so again as your guest, be sure that I will not wear garments which, before Byzantium was a village, were sacred to the gods of my country and those of my ancestors the Queens of Egypt.'"

"And then?" I asked.

"The Empress answered: 'Well spoken! Such would have been my own words had I been in your place. Moreover, they are true, and the robe becomes you well. Yet presume not too far, girl, seeing that Byzantium is no longer a village, and Egypt has some fanatic Moslem for a Pharaoh, who thinks little of your ancient blood.'

"So I bowed and went, and as I walked away heard the Empress rating the lady Martina about I know not what, save that your name came into the matter, and my own. Why does this Empress talk so much about you, Olaf, seeing that she has many officers who are higher in her service, and why was she so moved about this matter of the necklace of golden shells?"

"Heliodore," I answered, "I must tell now what I have hidden from you. The Augusta has been pleased—why, I cannot say, but chiefly, I suppose, because of late years it has been my fancy to keep myself apart from women, which is rare in this land—to show me certain favour. I gather, even, that, whether she means it or means it not, she has thought of me as a husband."

"Oh!" interrupted Heliodore, starting away from me, "now I understand everything. And, pray, have you thought as a wife of her, who has been a widow these ten years and has a son of twenty?"

"God above us alone knows what I have or have not thought, but it is certain that at present I think of her only as one who has been most kind to me, but who is more to be feared than my worst foe, if I have any."

"Hush!" she said, raising her finger. "I fancied I heard someone stir behind us."

"Fear nothing," I answered. "We are alone here, for I set guards of my own company around the place, with command to admit no one, and my order runs against all save the Empress in person."

"Then we are safe, Olaf, since this damp would disarrange her hair, which, I noted, is curled with irons, not by Nature, like my own. Oh! Olaf, Olaf, how wonderful is the fate that has brought us together. I say that when I saw you yonder in the cathedral for the first time since I was born, I knew you again, as you knew me. That is why, when you whispered to me, 'Greeting after the ages,' I gave you back your welcome. I know nothing of the past. If we lived and loved before, that tale is lost to me. But there's your dream and there's the necklace. When I was a child, Olaf, it was taken from the embalmed body of some royal woman, who, by tradition, was of my own race, yes, and by records of which my father can tell you, for he is among the last who can still read the writing of the old Egyptians. Moreover, she was very like me, Olaf, for I remember her well as she lay in her coffin, preserved by arts which the Egyptians had. She was young, not much older than I am to-day, and her story tells that she died in giving birth to a son, who grew up a strong and vigorous man, and although he was but half royal, founded a new dynasty in Egypt and became my forefather. This necklace lay upon her breast, and beneath it a writing on papyrus, which said that when the half of it which was lost should be joined again to that half, then those who had worn them would meet once more as mortals. Now the two halves of the necklace have met, and *we* have met as God decreed, and it is one and we are one for ever and for ever, let every Empress of the earth do what they will to part us."

"Aye," I answered, embracing her again, "we are one for ever and for ever, though perchance for a while we may be separated from time to time."

CHAPTER VII
VICTORY OR VALHALLA!

A minute later I heard a rustle as of branches being moved by people thrusting their way through them. A choked voice commanded,

"Take him living or dead."

Armed men appeared about us, four of them, and one cried "Yield!"

I sprang up and drew the Wanderer's sword.

"Who orders the General Michael to yield in his own command?" I asked.

"I do," answered the man. "Yield or die!"

Now, thinking that these were robbers or murderers hired by some enemy, I sprang at him, nor was that battle long, for at my first stroke he fell dead. Then the other three set on me. But I wore mail beneath my doublet, as Irene had bade me do, and their swords glanced. Moreover, the old northern rage entered into me, and these easterners were no match for my skill and strength. First one and then another of them went down, whereon the third fled away, taking with him a grizzly wound behind, for I struck him as he fled.

"Now it seems there is an end of that," I gasped to Heliodore, who was crouched upon the seat. "Come, let me take you to your father and summon my guards, ere we meet more of these murderers."

As I spoke a cloaked and hooded woman glided from the shelter of the trees behind and stood before us. She threw back the hood from her head and the moonlight fell upon her face. It was that of the Empress, but oh! so changed by jealous rage that I should scarce have known her. The large eyes seemed to flash fire, the cheeks were white, save where they had been touched with paint, the lips trembled. Twice she tried to speak and failed, but at the third effort words came.

"Nay, all is but begun," she said in a voice that was full of hate. "Know that I have heard your every word. So, traitor, you would tell my secrets to this Egyptian slut and then murder my own servants," and she pointed to the dead and wounded men. "Well, you shall pay for it, both of you, that I swear."

"Is it murder, Augusta," I asked, saluting, "when four assail one man, and, thinking them assassins, he fights for his life and wins the fray?"

"What are four such curs against you? I should have brought a dozen. Yet it was at me you struck. Whate'er they did I ordered them to do."

"Had I known it, Augusta, I would never have drawn sword, who am your officer and obedient to the end."

"Nay, you'd stab me with your tongue, not with your sword," she answered with something like a sob. "You say you are my obedient officer. Well, now we will see. Smite me that bold-faced baggage dead, or smite *me* dead, I care not which, then fall upon your sword."

"The first I cannot do, Augusta, for it would be murder against one who has done no wrong, and I will not stain my soul with murder."

"Done no wrong! Has she not mocked me, my years, my widowhood, yes, and even my hair, in the pride of her—her youth, me, the Empress of the World?"

Now Heliodore spoke for the first time.

"And has not the Empress of the World called a poor maid of blood as noble as her own by shameful names?" she asked.

"For the second," I went on before Irene could answer, "I cannot do that either, for it would be foul treason as well as murder to lift my sword against your anointed Majesty. But as for the third, as is my duty, that I will do—or rather suffer your servants to do—if it pleases you to repeat the order later when you are calm."

"What!" cried Heliodore, "would you go and leave me here? Then, Olaf, by the gods my forefathers worshipped for ten thousand years, and by the gods I worship, I'll find a means to follow you within an hour. Oh! Empress of the World, there is another world you do not rule, and there we'll call you to account."

Now Irene stared at Heliodore, and Heliodore stared back at her, and the sight was very strange.

"At least you have spirit, girl. But think not that shall save you, for there's no room for both of us on earth."

"If I go it may prove wide enough, Augusta," I broke in.

"Nay, you shall not go, Olaf, at least not yet. My orders are that you do *not* fall upon your sword. As for this Egyptian witch, well, presently my people will be here; then we will see."

Now I drew Heliodore to the trunk of the great tree which stood near by and set myself in front of her.

"What are you about to do?" asked the Empress.

"I am about to fight your eastern curs until I fall, for no northern man will lift a sword against me, even on your orders, Augusta. When I am down, this lady must play her own part as God shall guide her."

"Have no fear, Olaf," Heliodore said gently, "I wear a dagger."

Scarcely had she spoken when there was a sound of many feet. The man whom I had wounded had run shouting towards the palace, rousing the soldiers, both those on watch and those in their quarters. Now these began to arrive and to gather in the glade before the clump of trees, for some guards who had heard the clash of arms guided them to the place. They were of all races and sundry regiments, Greeks, Byzantines, Bulgars, Armenians, so-called Romans, and with them a number of Britons and northern men.

Seeing the Empress and, near by, myself standing with drawn sword against the tree sheltering the lady Heliodore, also on the ground those whom I had cut down, they halted. One of their officers asked what they must do.

"Kill me that man who has slain my servants, or stay—take him living," screamed the Augusta.

Now among those who had gathered was a certain lieutenant of my own, a blue-eyed, flaxen-haired Norwegian giant of the name of Jodd. This man loved me like a brother, I believe because once it had been my fortune to save his life. Also often I had proved his friend when he was in trouble, for in those days Jodd got drunk at times, and when he was drunk lost money which he could not pay.

Now, when he saw my case, I noted that this Jodd, who, if sober, was no fool at all, although he seemed so slow and stupid, whispered something to a comrade who was with him, whereon the man turned and fled away like an arrow. From the direction in which he went I guessed at once that he was running to the barracks close at hand, where were stationed quite three hundred Northmen, all of whom were under my command.

The soldiers prepared to obey the Augusta's orders, as they were bound to do. They drew their swords and a number of them advanced towards me slowly. Then it was that Jodd, with a few Northmen, moved between them and me, and, saluting the Empress, said in his bad Greek,

"Your pardon, Augusta, but why are we asked to kill our own general?"

"Obey my orders, fellow," she answered.

"Your pardon, Augusta," said the stolid Jodd, "but before we kill our own general, whom you commanded us to obey in all things, we would know why we must kill him. It is a custom of our country that no man shall be killed until he has been heard. General Olaf," and drawing his short sword for the first time, he saluted me in form, "be pleased to explain to us why you are to be killed or taken prisoner."

Now a tumult arose, and a eunuch in the background shouted to the soldiers to obey the Empress's orders, whereon again some of them began to advance.

"If no answer is given to my question," went on Jodd in his slow, bull-like voice, "I fear that others must be killed besides the General Olaf. Ho! Northmen. To me, Northmen! Ho! Britons, to me, Britons! Ho! Saxons, to me, Saxons! Ho! all who are not accursed Greeks. To me all who are not accursed Greeks!"

Now at each cry of Jodd's men leapt forward from the gathering crowd, and, to the number of fifty or more in all, marshalled themselves behind him, those of each nation standing shoulder to shoulder in little groups before me.

"Is my question to be answered?" asked Jodd. "Because, if not, although we be but one against ten, I think that ere the General Olaf is cut down or taken there will be good fighting this night."

Then I spoke, saying,

"Captain Jodd, and comrades, I will answer your question, and if I speak wrongly let the Augusta correct me. This is the trouble. The lady Heliodore here is my affianced wife. We were speaking together in this garden as the affianced do. The Empress, who, unseen by us, was hidden behind those trees, overheard our talk, which, for reasons best known to herself, for in it there was naught of treason or any matter of the State, made her so angry that she set her servants on to kill me. Thinking them murderers or robbers, I defended myself, and there they lie, save one, who fled away wounded. Then the Empress appeared and ordered me to kill the lady Heliodore. Comrades, look on her whom the Empress ordered me to kill, and say whether, were she your affianced, you would kill her even to please the Empress," and, stepping to one side, I showed them Heliodore in all her loveliness standing against the tree, the drawn dagger in her hand.

Now from those that Jodd had summoned there went up a roar of *"No,"* while even the rest were silent. Irene sprang forward and cried,

"Are my orders to be canvassed and debated? Obey! Cut this man down or take him living, I care not which, and with him all who cling to him, or to-morrow you hang, every one of you."

Now the soldiers who had gathered also began to form up under their officers, for they saw that before them was war and death. By this time they were many, and as the alarm spread minute by minute more arrived.

"Yield or we attack," said he who had taken command of them.

"I do not think that we yield," answered Jodd; and just then there came a sound of men running in ordered companies from the direction of the Northmen's barracks where Jodd's messenger had told his tale.

"I am *sure* that we do not yield," continued Jodd, and suddenly raised the wild northern war-cry, *"Valhalla, Valhalla! Victory or Valhalla!"*

Instantly from three hundred throats, above the sound of the running feet that drew ever nearer, came the answering shout of *"Valhalla, Valhalla! Victory or Valhalla!"* Then out of the gloom up dashed the Northmen.

Now other shouts arose of "Olaf! Olaf! Olaf! Where is our General Olaf? Where is Red-Sword?"

"Here, comrades!" roared Jodd, and up they came those fierce, bearded men, glad with the lust of battle, and ranged themselves by companies before us. Again the great voice of Jodd was heard, calling,

"Empress, do you give us Olaf and his girl and swear by your Christ that no harm shall come to them? Or must we take them for ourselves?"

"Never!" she cried back. "The only thing I give to you is death. On to these rebels, soldiers!"

Now, seeing what must come, I strove to speak, but Jodd shouted again,

"Be silent, Olaf. For this hour you are not our general; you are a prisoner whom it pleases us to rescue. Ring him round, Northmen, ring him round. Bring the Empress, too; she will serve as hostage."

Now some of them drew behind us. Then they began to advance, taking us along with them, and I, who was skilled in war, saw their purpose. They were drawing out into the open glade, where they could see to fight, and where their flanks would be protected by a stream of water on the one hand and a dense belt of trees on the other.

In her rage the Empress threw herself upon the ground, but two great fellows lifted her up by the arms and thrust her along with us. Marching thus, we reached the point that they had chosen, for the Greeks were in confusion and not ready to attack. There we halted, just on the crest of a little rise of ground.

"Augusta," I said, "in the name of God, I pray you to give way. These Northmen hate your Byzantines, and will take this chance to pay off their scores. Moreover, they love me, and will die to a man ere they see me harmed, and then how shall I protect you in the fray?"

She only glared at me and made no answer.

The attack began. By this time fifteen hundred or so of the Imperial troops had collected, and against them stood, perhaps, four hundred men in all, so that the odds were great. Still, they had no horsemen or archers, and our position was very good, also we were Northmen and they were Grecian scum.

On came the Byzantines, screaming "Irene! Irene!" in a formation of companies ranged one behind the other, for their object was to break in our centre by their weight. Jodd saw, and gave some orders; very good orders, I thought them. Then he sheathed his short-sword, seized the great battle-axe which was his favourite weapon, and placed himself in front of our triple line that waited in dead silence.

Up the slope surged the charge, and on the crest of it the battle met. At first the weight of the Greeks pressed us back, but, oh! they went down before the Northmen's steel like corn before the sickle, and soon that rush was stayed. Breast to breast they hewed and thrust, and so fearful was the fray that Irene, forgetting her rage, clung to me to protect her.

The fight hung doubtful. As in a dream, I watched the giant Jodd cut down a gorgeous captain, the axe shearing through his golden armour as though it were but silk. I watched a comrade of my own fall beneath a spear-thrust. I gazed at the face of Heliodore, who stared wide-eyed at the red scene, and at the white-lipped Irene, who was clinging to my arm. Now we were being pressed back again, we who at this point had at most two hundred men, some of whom were down, to bear the onslaught of twice that number, and, do what I would, my fingers strayed to my sword-hilt.

Our triple line bent in like a bow and began to break. The scales of war hung on the turn, when, from the dense belt of trees upon our left, suddenly rose the cry of "*Valhalla! Valhalla! Victory or Valhalla!*" for which I, who had overheard Jodd's orders, was waiting. These were his orders—that half of the Northmen should creep down behind the belt of trees in their dense shadow, and thus outflank the foe.

Forth they sprang by companies of fifty, the moonlight gleaming on their mail, and there, three hundred yards away, a new battle was begun. Now the Greeks in front of us, fearing for their rear, wavered a moment and fell back, perhaps, ten paces. I saw the opportunity and could bear no more, who before all things was a soldier.

Shouting to some of our wounded to watch the women, I drew my sword and leapt forward.

"I come, Northmen!" I cried, and was greeted with a roar of:

"Olaf Red-Sword! Follow Olaf Red-Sword!" for so the soldiers named me.

"Steady, Northmen! Shoulder to shoulder, Northmen!" I cried back. "Now at them! Charge! *Valhalla! Victory or Valhalla!*"

Down the slope they went before our rush. In thirty paces they were but a huddled mob, on which our swords played like lightnings. We rolled them back on to their supports, and those supports, outflanked, began to flee. We swept through and through them. We slew them by hundreds, we trod them beneath our victorious feet, and—oh! in that battle a strange thing happened to me. I thought I saw my dead brother Ragnar fighting at my side; aye, and I thought I heard him cry to me, in that lost, remembered voice:

"The old blood runs in you yet, you Christian man! Oh! you fight well, you Christian man. We of Valhalla give you greetings, Olaf Red-Sword. *Valhalla! Valhalla! Victory or Valhalla!*"

It was done. Some were fled, but more were dead, for, once at grips, the Northman showed no mercy to the Greek. Back we came, those who were left of us, for many, perhaps a hundred, were not, and formed a ring round the women and the wounded.

"Well done, Olaf," said Heliodore; but Irene only looked at me with a kind of wonder in her eyes.

Now the leaders of the Northmen began to talk among themselves, but although from time to time they glanced at me, they did not ask me to join in their talk. Presently Jodd came forward and said in his slow voice:

"Olaf Red-Sword, we love you, who have always loved us, your comrades, as we have shown you to-night. You have led us well, Olaf, and, considering our small numbers, we have just won a victory of which we are proud. But our necks are in the noose, as yours is, and we think that in this case our best course is to be bold. Therefore, we name you Cæsar. Having defeated the Greeks, we propose now to take the palace and to talk with the regiments without, many of whom are disloyal and shout for Constantine, whom after all they hate only a little less than they do Irene yonder. We know not what will be the end of the matter and do not greatly care, who set our fortunes upon a throw of the dice, but we think there is a good chance of victory. Do you accept, and will you throw in your sword with ours?"

"How can I," I answered, "when there stands the Empress, whose bread I have eaten and to whom I have sworn fealty?"

"An Empress, it seems, who desires to slay you over some matter that has to do with a woman. Olaf, the daggers of her assassins have cut this thread of fealty. Moreover, as it chances she is in our power, and as we cannot make our crime against her blacker than it is, we propose to rid you and ourselves of this Empress, who is our enemy, and who for her great wickedness well deserves to die. Such is our offer, to take or to leave, as time is short. Should you refuse it, we abandon you to your fate, and go to make our terms with Constantine, who also hates this Empress and even now is plotting her downfall."

As he spoke I saw certain men draw near to Irene for a purpose which I could guess, and stepped between her and them.

"The Augusta is my mistress," I said, "and although I attacked some of her troops but now, and she has wronged me much, still I defend her to the last."

"Little use in that, Olaf, seeing that you are but one and we are many," answered Jodd. "Come, will you be Cæsar, or will you not?"

Now Irene crept up behind me and whispered in my ear.

"Accept," she said. "It pleases me well. Be Cæsar as my husband. So you will save my life and my throne, of which I vow to you an equal share. With the help of your Northmen and the legions I command and who cling to me, we can defeat Constantine and rule the world together. This petty fray is nothing. What matters it if some lives have been lost in a palace tumult? The world lies in your grasp; take it, Olaf, and, with it, *me*."

I heard and understood. Now had come the great moment of my life. Something told me that on the one hand were majesty and empire; on the other much pain and sorrow yet with these a certain holy joy and peace. It was the latter that I chose, as doubtless Fate or God had decreed that I should do.

"I thank you, Augusta," I said, "but, while I can protect her, I will not seize a throne over the body of one who has been kind to me, nor will I buy it at the price you offer. There stands my predestined wife, and I can marry no other woman."

Now Irene turned to Heliodore, and said in a swift, low voice:

"Do you understand this matter, lady? Let us have done with jealousies and be plain, for the lives of all of us hang upon threads that, for some, must break within a day or two, and with them those of a thousand, thousand others. Aye, the destiny of the world is at stake. You say you love this man, whom I will tell you I love also. Well, if *you* win him, and he lives, which he scarce can hope to do, he gets your kisses in whatever corner of the earth will shelter him and you. If *I* win him, the empire of the earth is his. Moreover, girl," she added with meaning, "empresses are not always jealous; sometimes even they can look the other way. There would be high place for you within our Court, and, who knows? Your turn might come at length. Also your father's plans would be forwarded to the last pound of gold in our treasury and the last soldier in our service. Within five years, mayhap, he might rule Egypt as our Governor. What say you?"

Heliodore looked at the Empress with that strange, slow smile of hers. Then she looked at me, and answered:

"I say what Olaf says. There are two empires in the case. One, which you can give, Augusta, is of the world; the other, which I can give him here, is only a woman's heart, yet, as I think, of another eternal world that you do not know. I say what Olaf says. Let Olaf speak, Augusta."

"Empress," I said slowly, "again I thank you, but it may not be. My fate lies here," and I laid my hand upon the heart of Heliodore.

"You are mistaken, Olaf," answered the Empress, in a cold and quiet voice, but seemingly without anger; "your fate lies there," and she pointed to the ground, then added, "Believe me, I am sorry, for you are a man of whom any woman might be proud—yes, even an empress. I have always thought it, and I thought it again just now when I saw you lead that charge against those curs in armour," and she pointed towards the bodies of the Greeks. "So, it is finished, as perchance I am. If I must die, let it be on your sword, Olaf."

"Your answer, Olaf Red-Sword!" called Jodd. "You have talked enough."

"Your answer! Yes, your answer!" the Northmen echoed.

"The Empress has offered to share her crown with me, Jodd, but, friends, it cannot be, because of this lady to whom I am affianced."

"Marry them both," shouted a rude voice, but Jodd replied:

"Then that is soon settled. Out of our path, Olaf, and look the other way. When you turn your head again there will be no Empress to trouble you, except one of your own choosing."

On hearing these words, and seeing the swords draw near, Irene clutched hold of me, for always she feared death above everything.

"You will not see me butchered?" she gasped.

"Not while I live," I answered. "Hearken, friends. I am the general of the Augusta's guard, and if she dies, for honour's sake I must die first. Strike, then, if you will, but through my body."

"Tear her away!" called a voice.

"Comrades," I went on, "be not so mad. To-night we have done that which has earned us death, but while the Empress lives you have a hostage in your hands with whom you can buy pardon. As a lump of clay what worth is she to you? Hark! The regiments from the city!"

As I spoke, from the direction of the palace came a sound of many voices and of the tread of five thousand feet.

"True enough," said Jodd, with composure. "They are on us, and now it is too late to storm the palace. Olaf, like many another man, you have lost your chance of glory for a woman, or, who knows, perhaps you've won it. Well, comrades, as I take it you are not minded to fly and be hunted down like rats, only one thing remains—to die in a fashion they will remember in Byzantium. Olaf, you'd best mind the women; I will take command. Ring round, comrades, ring round! 'Tis a good place for it. Set the wounded in the middle. Keep that Empress living for the present, but when all is done, kill her. We'll be her escort to the gates of hell, for there she's bound if ever woman was."

Then, without murmur or complaint, almost in silence, indeed, they formed Odin's Ring, that triple circle of the Northmen doomed to die; the terrible circle that on many a battlefield has been hidden at last beneath the heap of fallen foes.

The regiments moved up; there were three of them of full strength. Irene stared about her, seeking some loophole of escape, and finding none. Heliodore and I talked together in low tones, making our tryst beyond the grave. The regiments halted within fifty paces of us. They liked not the look of Odin's Ring, and the ground over which they had marched and the fugitives with whom they had spoken told them that many of them looked their last upon the moon.

Some mounted generals rode towards us and asked who was in command of the Northmen. When they learned that it was Jodd, they invited him to a parley. The end of it was that Jodd and two others stepped twenty paces from our ranks, and met a councillor—it was Stauracius—and two of the generals in the open, where no treachery could well be practised, especially as Stauracius was not a man of war. Here they talked together for a long while. Then Jodd and his companions returned, and Jodd said, so that all might hear him:

"Hearken. These are the terms offered: That we return to our barracks in peace, bearing our weapons. That nothing be laid to our charge under any law, military or civil, by the State or private persons, for this night's slaying and tumult, and that in guarantee thereof twelve hostages of high rank, upon whose names we have agreed, be given into our keeping. That we retain our separate stations in the service of the Empire, or have leave to quit that service within three months, with the gratuity of a quarter's pay, and go where we will unmolested. But that, in return for these boons, we surrender the person of the Empress unharmed, and with her that of the General Olaf, to whom a fair trial is promised before a military court. That with her own voice the Augusta shall confirm all these undertakings before she leaves our ranks. Such is the offer, comrades."

"And if we refuse it, what?" asked a voice.

"This: That we shall be ringed round, and either starved out or shot down by archers. Or, if we try to escape, that we shall be overwhelmed by numbers, and any of us who chance to be taken living shall be hanged, sound and wounded together."

Now the leaders of the Northmen consulted. Irene watched them for awhile, then turned to me and asked,

"What will they do, Olaf?"

"I cannot say, Augusta," I answered, "but I think that they will offer to surrender you and not myself, since they may doubt them of that fair trial which is promised to me."

"Which means," she said, "that, whether I live or die, all these brave men will be sacrificed to you, Olaf, who, after all, must perish with them, as will this Egyptian. Are you prepared to accept that blood-offering, Olaf? If so, you must have changed from the man I loved."

"No, Augusta," I answered, "I am not prepared. Rather would I trust myself into your power, Augusta."

The conference of the officers had come to an end. Their leader advanced and said,

"We accept the terms, except as to the matter of Olaf Red-Sword. The Empress may go free, but Olaf Red-Sword, our general whom we love, we will not surrender. First will we die."

"Good!" said Jodd. "I looked for such words from you."

Then he marched out, with his companions, and again met Stauracius and the two generals of the Greeks. After they had talked a little while he returned and said,

"Those two officers, being men, would have agreed, but Stauracius, the eunuch, who seems in command, will not agree. He says that Olaf Red-Sword must be surrendered with the Empress. We answered that in this case soon there would be no Empress to surrender except one ready for burial. He replied that was as God might decree; either both must be surrendered or both be held."

"Do you know why the dog said that?" whispered Irene to me. "It was because those Northmen have let slip the offer I made to you but now, and he is jealous of you, and fears you may take his power. Well, if I live, one day he shall pay for this who cares so little for my life."

So she spoke, but I made no answer. Instead, I turned to Heliodore, saying,

"You see how matters stand, beloved. Either I must surrender myself, or all these brave men must perish, and we with them. For myself, I am ready to die, but I am not willing that you and they should die. Also, if I yield, I can do no worse than die, whereas perchance after all things will take another turn. Now what say you?"

"I say, follow your heart, Olaf," she replied steadily. "Honour comes first of all. The rest is with God. Wherever you go there I soon shall be."

"I thank you," I answered; "your mind is mine."

Then I stepped forward and said,

"Comrades, it is my turn to throw in this great game. I have heard and considered all, and I think it best that I should be surrendered, with the Augusta, to the Greeks."

"We will not surrender you," they shouted.

"Comrades, I am still your general, and my order is that you surrender me. Also, I have other orders to give to you. That you guard this lady Heliodore to the last, and that, while one of you remains alive, she shall be to you as though she were that man's daughter, or mother, or sister, to help and protect as best he may in every circumstance, seen or unforeseen. Further, that with her you guard her father, the noble Egyptian Magas. Will you promise this to me?"

"Aye!" they roared in answer.

"You hear them, Heliodore," I said. "Know that henceforth you are one of a large family, and, however great your enemies, that you will never lack a friend. Comrades," I went on, "this is my second order, and perchance the last that I shall ever give to you. Unless you hear that I am evilly treated in the palace yonder, stay quiet. But if that tidings should reach you, then all oaths are broken. Do what you can and will."

"Aye!" they roared again.

Afterwards what happened? It comes back to me but dimly. I think they swore the Empress on the Blood of Christ that I should go unharmed. I think I embraced Heliodore before them all, and gave her into their keeping. I think I whispered into the ear of Jodd to seek out the Bishop Barnabas, and pray him to get her and her father away to Egypt without delay—yes, even by force, if it were needful. Then I think I left their lines, and that, as I went, leading the Augusta by the hand, they gave to me the general's salute. That I turned and saluted them in answer ere I yielded myself into the power of my god-father, Stauracius, who greeted me with a false and sickly smile.

CHAPTER VIII
THE TRIAL OF OLAF

I know not what time went by before I was put upon my trial, but that trial I can still see as clearly as though it were happening before my eyes. It took place in a long, low room of the vast palace buildings that was lighted only by window-places set high up in the wall. These walls were frescoed, and at the end of the room above the seat of the judges was a rude picture in bright colours of the condemnation of Christ by Pilate. Pilate, I remember, was represented with a black face, to signify his wickedness I suppose, and in the air above him hung a red-eyed imp shaped like a bat who gripped his robe with one claw and whispered into his ear.

There were seven judges, he who presided being a law-officer, and the other six captains of different grades, chosen mostly from among the survivors of those troops whom the Northmen had defeated on the night of the battle in the palace gardens. As this was a military trial, I was allowed no advocate to defend me, nor indeed did I ask for any. The Court, however, was open and crowded with spectators, among whom I saw most of the great officers of the palace, Stauracius with them; also some ladies, one of whom was Martina, my god-mother. The back of the long room was packed with soldiers and others, not all of whom were my enemies.

Into this place I was brought, guarded by four negroes, great fellows armed with swords whom I knew to be chosen out of the number of the executioners of the palace and the city. Indeed, one of them had served under me when I was governor of the State prison, and been dismissed by me because of some cruelty which he had practised.

Noting all these things and the pity in Martina's eyes, I knew that I was already doomed, but as I had expected nothing else this did not trouble me over much.

I stood before the judges, and they stared at me.

"Why do you not salute us, fellow?" asked one of them, a mincing Greek captain whom I had seen running like a hare upon the night of the fray.

"Because, Captain, I am of senior rank to any whom I see before me, and as yet uncondemned. Therefore, if salutes are in the question, it is you who should salute me."

At this speech they stared at me still harder than before, but among the soldiers at the end of the hall there arose something like a murmur of applause.

"Waste no time in listening to his insolence," said the president of the Court. "Clerk, set out the case."

Then a black-robed man who sat beneath the judges rose and read the charge to me from a parchment. It was brief and to the effect that I, Michael, formerly known as Olaf or Olaf Red-Sword, a Northman in the service of the Empress Irene, a general in her armies, a chamberlain and Master of the Palace, had conspired against the Empress, had killed her servants, had detained her person, threatening to murder her; had made war upon her troops and slain some hundreds of them by the help of other Northmen, and wounded many more.

I was asked what I pleaded to this charge, and replied,

"I am not guilty."

Then witnesses were called. The first of these was the fourth man whom Irene had set upon me, who alone escaped with a wound behind. This fellow, having been carried into court, for he could not walk, leaned over a bar, for he could not sit down, and told his story. When he had finished I was allowed to examine him.

"Why did the Empress order you and your companions to attack me?" I asked.

"I think because she saw you kiss the Egyptian lady, General," at which answer many laughed.

"You tried to kill me, did you not?"

"Yes, General, for the Empress ordered us so to do."

"Then what happened?"

"You killed or cut down three of us one after the other, General, being too skilful and strong for us. As I turned to fly, me you wounded here," and, dragging himself round with difficulty, he showed how my sword had fallen on a part where no soldier should receive a wound. At this sight those in the Court laughed again.

"Did I provoke you in any way before you attacked me?"

"No, indeed, General. It was the Empress you provoked by kissing the beautiful Egyptian lady. At least, I think so, since every time you kissed each other she seemed to become more mad, and at last ordered us to kill both of you."

Now the laughter grew very loud, for even the Court officers could no longer restrain themselves, and the ladies hid their faces in their hands and tittered.

"Away with that fool!" shouted the president of the Court, and the poor fellow was hustled out. What became of him afterwards I do not know, though I can guess.

Now appeared witness after witness who told of the fray which I have described already, though for the most part they tried to put another colour on the matter. Of many of these men I asked no questions. Indeed, growing weary of their tales, I said at length to the judges,

"Sirs, what need is there for all this evidence, seeing that among you I perceive three gallant officers whom I saw running before the Northmen that night, when with some four hundred swords we routed about two thousand of you? You yourselves, therefore, are the best witnesses of what befell. Moreover, I acknowledge that, being moved by the sight of war, in the end I led the charge against you, before which charge some died and many fled, you among them."

Now these captains glowered at me and the president said,

"The prisoner is right. What need is there of more evidence?"

"I think much, sir," I answered, "since but one side of the story has been heard. Now I will call witnesses, of whom the first should be the Augusta, if she is willing to appear and tell you what happened within the circle of the Northmen on that night."

"Call the Augusta!" gasped the president. "Perchance, prisoner Michael, you will wish next to call God Himself on your behalf?"

"That, sir," I answered, "I have already done and do. Moreover," I added slowly, "of this I am sure, that in a time to come, although it be not to-morrow or the next day, you and everyone who has to do with this case will find that I have not called Him in vain."

At these words for a few moments a solemn silence fell upon the Court. It was as though they had gone home to the heart of everyone who was present there. Also I saw the curtains that draped a gallery high up in the wall shake a little. It came into my mind that Irene herself was hidden behind those curtains, as afterwards I learned was the case, and that she had made some movement which caused them to tremble.

"Well," said the president, after this pause, "as God does not appear to be your witness, and as you have no other, seeing that you cannot give evidence yourself under the law, we will now proceed to judgment."

"Who says that the General Olaf, Olaf Red-Sword, has no witness?" exclaimed a deep voice at the end of the hall. "I am here to be his witness."

"Who speaks?" asked the president. "Let him come forward."

There was a disturbance at the end of the hall, and through the crowd that he seemed to throw before him to right and left appeared the mighty form of Jodd. He was clad in full armour and bore his famous battle-axe in his hand.

"One whom some of you know well enough, as others of your company who will never know anything again have done in the past. One named Jodd, the Northman, second in command of the guard to the General Olaf," he answered, and marched to the spot where witnesses were accustomed to stand.

"Take away that barbarian's axe," exclaimed an officer who sat among the judges.

"Aye," said Jodd, "come hither, mannikin, and take it away if you can. I promise you that along with it something else shall be taken away, to wit your fool's head. Who are you that would dare to disarm an officer of the Imperial Guard?"

After this there was no more talk of removing Jodd's axe, and he proceeded to give his evidence, which, as it only detailed what has been written already, need not be repeated. What effect it produced upon the judges, I cannot say, but that it moved those present in the Court was clear enough.

"Have you done?" asked the president at length when the story was finished.

"Not altogether," said Jodd. "Olaf Red-Sword was promised an open trial, and that he has, since otherwise I and some friends of mine could not be in this Court to tell the truth, where perhaps the truth has seldom been heard before. Also he was promised a fair trial, and that he has not, seeing that the most of his judges are men with whom he fought the other day and who only escaped his sword by flight. To-morrow I propose to ask the people of Byzantium whether it is right that a man should be tried by his conquered enemies. Now I perceive that you will find a verdict of 'guilty' against Olaf Red-Sword, and perhaps condemn him to death. Well, find what verdict you will and pass what sentence you will, but do not dare to attempt to execute that sentence."

"Dare! Dare!" shouted the president. "Who are you, man, who would dictate to a Court appointed by the Empress what it shall or shall not do? Be careful lest we pass sentence on you as well as on your fellow-traitor. Remember where you stand, and that if I lift my finger you will be taken and bound."

"Aye, lawyer, I remember this and other things. For instance, that I have the safe-conduct of the Empress under an oath sworn on the Cross of the Christ she worships. For instance, also, that I have three hundred comrades waiting my safe return."

"Three hundred!" snarled the president. "The Empress has three thousand within these walls who will soon make an end of your three hundred."

"I have been told, lawyer," answered Jodd, "that once there lived another monarch, one called Xerxes, who thought that he would make an end of a certain three hundred Greeks, when Greeks were different from what you are to-day, at a place called Thermopylæ. He made an end of them, but they cost him more than he cared to pay, and now it is those Greeks who live for ever and Xerxes who is dead. But that's not all; since that fray the other night we Northmen have found friends. Have you heard of the Armenian legions, President, those who favour Constantine? Well, kill Olaf Red-Sword, or kill me, Jodd, and you have to deal first with the Northmen and next with the Armenian legions. Now here I am waiting to be taken by any who can pass this axe."

At these words a great silence fell upon the Court. Jodd glared about him, and, seeing that none ventured to draw near, stepped from the witness-place, advanced to where I was, gave me the full salute of ceremony, then marched away to the back of the Court, the crowd opening a path for him.

When he had gone the judges began to consult together, and, as I expected, very soon agreed upon their verdict. The president said, or rather gabbled,

"Prisoner, we find you guilty. Have you any reason to offer why sentence of death should not be passed upon you?"

"Sir," I answered, "I am not here to plead for my life, which already I have risked a score of times in the service of your people. Yet I would say this. On the night of the outbreak I was set on, four to one, for no crime, as you have heard, and did but protect myself. Afterwards, when I was about to be slain, the Northmen, my comrades, protected me unasked; then I did my best to save the life of the Empress, and, in fact, succeeded. My only offence is that when the great charge took place and your regiments were defeated, remembering only that I was a soldier, I led that charge. If this is a crime worthy of death, I am ready to die. Yet I hold that both God and man will give more honour to me the criminal than to you the judges, and to those who before ever you sat in this Court instructed you, whom I know to be but tools, as to the verdict that you should give."

The applause which my words called forth from those gathered at the end of the Court died away. In the midst of a great silence the president, who, like his companions, I could see well, was growing somewhat fearful, read the sentence in a low voice from a parchment. After setting out the order by which the Court was constituted and other matters, it ran:

"We condemn you, Michael, otherwise called Olaf or Olaf Red-Sword, to death. This sentence will be executed with or without torture at such time and in such manner as it may please the Augusta to decree."

Now the voice of Jodd was heard crying through the gathering gloom, for night was near:

"What sort of judgment is this that the judges bring already written down into the Court? Hearken you, lawyer, and you street-curs, his companions, who call yourselves soldiers. If Olaf Red-Sword dies, those hostages whom we hold die also. If he is tortured, those hostages will be tortured also. Moreover, ere long we will sack this fine place, and what has befallen Olaf shall befall you also, you false judges, neither less nor more. Remember it, all you who shall have charge of Olaf in his bonds, and, if she be within hearing, let the Augusta Irene remember it also, lest another time there should be no Olaf to save her life."

Now I could see that the judges were terrified. Hastily, with white faces, they consulted together as to whether they should order Jodd to be seized. Presently I heard the president say to his companions:

"Nay, best let him go. If he is touched, our hostages will die. Moreover, doubtless Constantine and the Armenians are at the back of him, or he would not dare to speak thus. Would that we were clear of this business which has been thrust upon us."

Then he called aloud, "Let the prisoner be removed."

Down the long Court I was marched, only now guards, who had been called in, went in front of and behind me, and with them the four executioners by whom I was surrounded.

"Farewell, god-mother," I whispered to Martina as I passed.

"Nay, not farewell," she whispered back, looking up at me with eyes that were full of tears, though what she meant I did not know.

At the end of the Court, where those who dared to sympathise with me openly were gathered, rough voices called blessings on me and rough hands patted me on the shoulder. To one of these men whose voice I recognised in the gloom I turned to speak a word. Thereon the black executioner who was between us, he whom I had dismissed from the jail for cruelty, struck me on the mouth with the back of his hand. Next instant I heard a sound that reminded me of the growl the white bear gave when it gripped Steinar. Two arms shot out and caught that black savage by the head. There was a noise as of something breaking, and down went the man—a corpse.

Then they hurried me away, for now it was not only the judges who were afraid.

It comes to me that for some days, three or four, I sat in my cell at the palace, for here I was kept because, as I learned afterwards, it was feared that if I were removed to that State prison of which I had been governor, some attempt would be made to rescue me.

This cell was one of several situated beneath that broad terrace which looked out on to the sea, where Irene had first questioned me as to the shell necklace and, against my prayer, had set it upon her own breast. It had a little barred window, out of which I could watch the sea, and through this window came the sound of sentries tramping overhead and of the voice of the officer who, at stated hours, arrived to turn out the guard, as for some years it had been my duty to do.

I wondered who that officer might be, and wondered also how many of such men since Byzantium became the capital of the Empire had filled his office and mine, and what had become of them all. As I knew, if that terrace had been able to speak, it could have told many bloody histories, whereof doubtless mine would be another. Doubtless, too, there were more to follow until the end came, whatever that might be.

In that strait place I reflected on many things. All my youth came back to me. I marvelled what had happened at Aar since I left it such long years ago. Once or twice rumours had reached me from men in my company, who were Danish-born, that Iduna was a great lady there and still unmarried. But of Freydisa I had heard nothing. Probably she was dead, and, if so, I felt sure that her fierce and faithful spirit must be near me now, as that of Ragnar had seemed to be in the Battle of the Garden.

How strange it was that after all my vision had been fulfilled and it had been my lot to meet her of whom I had dreamed, wearing that necklace of which I had found one-half upon the Wanderer in his grave-mound. Were I and the Wanderer the same spirit, I asked of myself, and she of the dream and Heliodore the same woman?

Who could tell? At least this was sure, from the moment that first we saw one another we knew we belonged each to each for the present and the future. Therefore, as it was with these we had to do, the past might sleep and all its secrets.

Now we had met but to be parted again by death, which seemed hard indeed. Yet since we *had* met, for my part Fate had my forgiveness for I knew that we should meet again. I looked back on what I had done and left undone, and could not blame myself overmuch. True, it would have been wiser if I had stayed by Irene and Heliodore, and not led that charge against the Greeks. Only then, as a soldier, I should never have forgiven myself, for how could I stand still while my comrades fought for me? No, no, I was glad I had led the charge and led it well, though my life must pay its price. Nor was this so. I must die, not because I had lifted sword against Irene's troops, but for the sin of loving Heliodore.

After all, what was life as we knew it? A passing breath! Well, as the body breathes many million times between the cradle and the grave, so I believed the soul must breathe out its countless lives, each ending in a form of death. And beyond these, what? I did not know, yet my new-found faith gave me much comfort.

In such meditations and in sleep I passed my hours, waiting always until the door of my cell should open and through it appear, not the jailer with my food, which I noted was plentiful and delicate, but the executioners or mayhap the tormentors.

At length it did open, somewhat late at night, just as I was about to lay myself down to rest, and through it came a veiled woman. I bowed and motioned to my visitor to be seated on the stool that was in the cell, then waited in silence. Presently she threw off her veil, and in the light of the lamp showed that I stood before the Empress Irene.

"Olaf," she said hoarsely, "I am come here to save you from yourself, if it may be so. I was hidden in yonder Court, and heard all that passed at your trial."

"I guessed as much, Augusta," I said, "but what of it?"

"For one thing, this: The coward and fool, who now is dead—of his wounds—who gave evidence as to the killing of the three other cowards by you, has caused my name to become a mock throughout Constantinople. Aye, the vilest make songs upon me in the streets, such songs as I cannot repeat."

"I am grieved, Augusta," I said.

"It is I who should grieve, not you, who are told of as a man who grew weary of the love of an Empress, and cast her off as though she were a tavern wench. That is the first matter. The second is that under the finding of the Court of Justice——"

"Oh! Augusta," I interrupted, "why stain your lips with those words 'of justice'!"

"——Under the finding of the Court," she went on, "your fate is left in my hands. I may kill you or torment your body. Or I may spare you and raise your head higher than any other in the Empire, aye, and adorn it with a crown."

"Doubtless you may do any of these things, Augusta, but which of them do you wish to do?"

"Olaf, notwithstanding all that has gone, I would still do the last. I speak to you no more of love or tenderness, nor do I pretend that this is for your sake alone. It is for mine also. My name is smirched, and only marriage can cover up the stain upon it. Moreover, I am beset by troubles and by dangers. Those accursed Northmen, who love you so well and who fight, not like men but like devils, are in league with the Armenian legions and with Constantine. My generals and my troops fall away from me. If it were assailed, I am not sure that I could hold this palace, strong though it be. There's but one man who can make me safe again, and that man is yourself. The Northmen will do your bidding, and with you in command of them I fear no attack. You have the honesty, the wit and the soldier's skill and courage. You must command, or none. Only this time it must not be as Irene's lover, for that is what they name you, but as her husband. A priest is waiting within call, and one of high degree. Within an hour, Olaf, you may be my consort, and within a year the Emperor of the World. Oh!" she went on with passion, "cannot you forgive what seem to be my sins when you remember that they were wrought for love of you?"

"Augusta," I said, "I have small ambition; I am not minded to be an emperor. But hearken. Put aside this thought of marriage with one so far beneath you, and let me marry her whom I have chosen, and who has chosen me. Then once more I'll take command of the Northmen and defend you and your cause to the last drop of my blood."

Her face hardened.

"It may not be," she said, "not only for those reasons I have told you, but for another which I grieve to have to tell. Heliodore, daughter of Magas the Egyptian, is dead.'

"Dead!" I gasped. "Dead!"

"Aye, Olaf, dead. You did not see, and she, being a brave woman, hid it from you, but one of those spears that were flung in the fight struck her in the side. For a while the wound went well. But two days ago it mortified; last night she died and this morning I myself saw her buried with honour."

"How did you see her buried, you who are not welcome among the Northmen?" I asked.

"By my order, as her blood was high, she was laid in the palace graveyard, Olaf."

"Did she leave me no word or token, Augusta? She swore to me that if she died she would send to me the other half of that necklace which I wear."

"I have heard of none," said Irene, "but you will know, Olaf, that I have other business to attend to just now than such death-bed gossip. These things do not come to my ears."

I looked at Irene and Irene looked at me.

"Augusta," I said, "I do not believe your story. No spear wounded Heliodore while I was near her, and when I was not near her your Greeks were too far away for any spears to be thrown. Indeed, unless you stabbed her secretly, she was not wounded, and I am sure that, however much you have hated her, this you would not have dared to do for your own life's sake. Augusta, for your own purposes you are trying to deceive me. I will not marry you. Do your worst. You have lied to me about the woman whom I love, and though I forgive you all the rest, this I do not forgive. You know well that Heliodore still lives beneath the sun."

"If so," answered the Empress, "you have looked your last upon the sun and—her. Never again shall you behold the beauty of Heliodore. Have you aught to say? There is still time."

"Nothing, Augusta, at present, except this. Of late I have learned to believe in a God. I summon you to meet me before that God. There we will argue out our case and abide His judgment. If there is no God there will be no judgment, and I salute you, Empress, who triumph. If, as I believe and as you say you believe, there is a God, think whom *you* will be called upon to salute when that God has heard the truth. Meanwhile I repeat that Heliodore the Egyptian still lives beneath the sun."

Irene rose from the stool on which she sat and thought a moment. I gazed through the bars of the window-place in my cell out at the night above. A young moon was floating in the sky, and near to it hung a star. A little passing cloud with a dented edge drifted over the star and the lower horn of the moon. It went by, and they shone out again upon the background of the blue heavens. Also an owl flitted across the window-place of my cell. It had a mouse in its beak, and the shadow of it and of the writhing mouse for a moment lay upon Irene's breast, for I turned my head and saw them. It came into my mind that here was an allegory. Irene was the night-hawk, and I was the writhing mouse that fed its appetite. Doubtless it was decreed that the owl must be and the mouse must be, but beyond them both, hidden in those blue heavens, stood that Justice which we call God.

These were the last things that I saw in this life of mine, and therefore I remember them well, or rather, almost the last. The very last of which I took note was Irene's face. It had grown like to that of a devil. The great eyes in it stared out between the puffed and purple eyelids. The painted cheeks had sunk in and were pallid beneath and round the paint. The teeth showed in two white lines, the chin worked. She was no longer a beautiful woman, she was a fiend.

Irene knocked thrice upon the door. Bolts were thrown back, and men entered.

"Blind him!" she said.

CHAPTER IX
THE HALL OF THE PIT

The days and the nights went by, but which was day and which was night I knew not, save for the visits of the jailers with my meals—I who was blind, I who should never see the light again. At first I suffered much, but by degrees the pain died away. Also a physician came to tend my hurts, a skilful man. Soon I discovered, however, that he had another object. He pitied my state, so much, indeed, he said, that he offered to supply me with a drug that, if I were willing to take it, would make an end of me painlessly. Now I understood at once that Irene desired my death, and, fearing to cause it, set the means of self-murder within my reach.

I thanked the man and begged him to give me the drug, which he did, whereon I hid it away in my garments. When it was seen that I still lived although I had asked for the medicine, I think that Irene believed this was because it had failed to work, or that such a means of death did not please me. So she found another. One evening when a jailer brought my supper he pressed something heavy into my hand, which I felt to be a sword.

"What weapon is this?" I asked, "and why do you give it to me?"

"It is your own sword," answered the man, "which I was commanded to return to you. I know no more."

Then he went away, leaving the sword with me.

I drew the familiar blade from its sheath, the red blade that the Wanderer had worn, and touching its keen edge with my fingers, wept from my blinded eyes to think that never again could I hold it aloft in war or see the light flash from it as I smote. Yes, I wept in my weakness, till I remembered that I had no longer any wish to be the death of men. So I sheathed the good sword and hid it beneath my mattress lest some jailer should steal it, which, as I could not see him, he might do easily. Also I desired to put away temptation.

I think that this hour after the bringing of the sword, which stirred up so many memories, was the most fearful of all my hours, so fearful that, had it been prolonged, death would have come to me of its own accord. I had sunk to misery's lowest deep, who did not know that even then its tide was turning, who could not dream of all the blessed years that lay before me, the years of love and of such peaceful joy as even the blind may win.

That night Martina came—Martina, who was Hope's harbinger. I heard the door of my prison open and close softly, and sat still, wondering whether the murderers had entered at last, wondering, too, whether I should snatch the sword and strike blindly till I fell. Next I heard another sound, that of a woman weeping; yes, and felt my hand lifted and pressed to a woman's lips, which kissed it again and yet again. A thought struck me, and I began to draw it back. A soft voice spoke between its sobs.

"Have no fear, Olaf. I am Martina. Oh, now I understand why yonder tigress sent me on that distant mission."

"How did you come here, Martina?" I asked.

"I still have the signet, Olaf, which Irene, who begins to mistrust me, forgets. Only this morning I learned the truth on my return to the palace; yet I have not been idle. Within an hour Jodd and the Northmen knew it also. Within three they had blinded every hostage whom they held, aye, and caught two of the brutes who did the deed on you, and crucified them upon their barrack walls."

"Oh! Martina," I broke in, "I did not desire that others who are innocent should share my woes."

"Nor did I, Olaf; but these Northmen are ill to play with. Moreover, in a sense it was needful. You do not know what I have learned—that to-morrow Irene proposed to slit your tongue also because you can tell too much, and afterwards to cut off your right hand lest you, who are learned, should write down what you know. I told the Northmen—never mind how. They sent a herald, a Greek whom they had captured, and, covering him with arrows, made him call out that if your tongue was slit they would know of it and slit the tongues of all the hostages also, and that if your hand was cut off they could cut off their hands, and take another vengeance which for the present they keep secret."

"At least they are faithful," I said. "But, oh! tell me, Martina, what of Heliodore?"

"This," she whispered into my ear. "Heliodore and her father sailed an hour after sunset and are now safe upon the sea, bound for Egypt."

"Then I was right! When Irene told me she was dead she lied."

"Aye, if she said that she lied, though thrice she has striven to murder her, I have no time to tell you how, but was always baffled by those who watched. Yet she might have succeeded at last, so, although Heliodore fought against it, it was best that she should go. Those who are parted may meet again; but how can we meet one who is dead until we too are dead?"

"How did she go?"

"Smuggled from the city disguised as a boy attending on a priest, and that priest her father shorn of his beard and tonsured. The Bishop Barnabas passed them out in his following."

"Then blessings on the Bishop Barnabas," I said.

"Aye, blessings on him, since without his help it could never have been done. The secret agents at the port stared hard at those two, although the good bishop vouched for them and gave their names and offices. Still, when they saw some rough-looking fellows dressed like sailors approach, playing with the handles of their knives, the agents thought well to ask no more questions. Moreover, now that the ship has sailed, for their own sakes they'll swear that no such priest and boy went aboard of her. So your Heliodore is away unharmed, as is her father, though his mission has come to naught. Still, his life is left in him, for which he may be thankful, who on such a business should have brought no woman. If he had come alone, Olaf, your eyes would have been left to you, and set by now upon the orb of empire that your hand had grasped."

"Yet I am glad that he did not come alone, Martina."

"Truly you have a high and faithful heart, and that woman should be honoured whom you love. What is the secret? There must be more in it than the mere desire for a woman's beauty, though I know that at times this can make men mad. In such a business the soul must play its part."

"I think so, Martina. Indeed, I believe so, since otherwise we suffer much in vain. Now tell me, how and when do I die?"

"I hope you will not die at all, Olaf. Certain plans are laid which even here I dare not whisper. To-morrow I hear they will lead you again before the judges, who, by Irene's clemency, will change your sentence to one of banishment, with secret orders to kill you on the voyage. But you will never make that voyage. Other schemes are afoot; you'll learn of them afterwards."

"Yet, Martina, if you know these plots the Augusta knows them also, since you and she are one."

"When those dagger points were thrust into your eyes, Olaf, they cut the thread that bound us, and now Irene and I are more far apart than hell and heaven. I tell you that for your sake I hate her and work her downfall. Am I not your god-mother, Olaf?"

Then again she kissed my hand and presently was gone.

On the following morning, as I supposed it to be, my jailers came and said to me that I must appear before the judges to hear some revision of my sentence. They dressed me in my soldier's gear, and even allowed me to gird my sword about me, knowing, doubtless, that, save to himself, a blind man could do no mischief with a sword. Then they led me I know not whither by passages which turned now here, now there. At length we entered some place, for doors were closed behind us.

"This is the Hall of Judgment," said one of them, "but the judges have not yet come. It is a great room and bare. There is nothing in it against which you can hurt yourself. Therefore, if it pleases you after being cramped so long in that narrow cell, you may walk to and fro, keeping your hands in front of you so that you will know when you touch the further wall and must turn."

I thanked them and, glad enough to avail myself of this grace for my limbs were stiff with want of exercise, began to walk joyfully. I thought that the room must be one of those numberless apartments which opened on to the terrace, since distinctly I could hear the wash of the sea coming from far beneath, doubtless through the open window-places.

Forward I stepped boldly, but at a certain point in my march this curious thing happened. A hand seemed to seize my own and draw me to the left. Wondering, I followed the guidance of the hand, which presently left hold of mine. Thereon I continued my march, and as I did so, thought that I heard another sound, like to that of a suppressed murmur of human voices. Twenty steps more and I reached the end of the chamber, for my outstretched fingers touched its marble wall. I turned and marched back, and lo! at the twentieth step that hand took mine again and led me to the right, whereon once more the murmur of voices reached me.

Thrice this happened, and every time the murmur grew more loud. Indeed, I thought I heard one say,

"The man's not blind at all," and another, "Some spirit guides him."

As I made my fourth journey I caught the sound of a distant tumult, the shouts of war, the screams of agony, and above them all the well-remembered cry of "Valhalla! Valhalla! Victory or Valhalla!"

I halted where I was and felt the blood rush into my wasted cheeks. The Northmen, my Northmen, were in the palace! It was at this that Martina had hinted. Yet in so vast a place what chance was there that they would ever find me, and how, being blind, could I find them? Well, at least my voice was left to me, and I would lift it.

So with all my strength I cried aloud, "Olaf Red-Sword is here! To Olaf, men of the North!"

Thrice I cried. I heard folk running, not to me, but from me, doubtless those whose whispers had reached my ears.

I thought of trying to follow them, but the soft and gentle hand, which was like to that of a woman, once more clasped mine and held me where I was, suffering me to move no single inch. So there I stood, even after the hand had loosed me again, for it seemed to me that there was something most strange in this business.

Presently another sound arose, the sound of the Northmen pouring towards the hall, for feet clanged louder and louder down the marble corridors. More, they had met those who were running from the hall, for now these fled back before them. They were in the hall, for a cry of horror, mingled with rage, broke from their lips.

"'Tis Olaf," said one, "Olaf blinded, and, by Thor, see where he stands!"

Then Jodd's voice roared out,

"Move not, Olaf; move not, or you die."

Another voice, that of Martina, broke in, "Silence, you fool, or you'll frighten him and make him fall. Silence all, and leave him to me!"

Then quiet fell upon the place; it seemed that even the pursued grew quiet, and I heard the rustle of a woman's dress drawing towards me. Next instant a soft hand took my own, just such a hand as not long ago had seemed to guide and hold me, and Martina's voice said,

"Follow where I lead, Olaf."

So I followed eight or ten paces. Then Martina threw her arms about me and burst into wild laughter. Someone caught her away; next moment two hair-clad lips kissed me on the brow and the mighty voice of Jodd shouted,

"Thanks be to all the gods, dwell they in the north or in the south! We have saved you! Know you where you stood, Olaf? On the brink of a pit, the very brink, and beneath is a fall of a hundred feet to where the waters of the Bosphorus wash among the rocks. Oh! understand this pretty Grecian game. They, good Christian folk, would not have your blood upon their souls, and therefore they caused you to walk to your own death. Well, they shall be dosed with the draught they brewed.

"Bring them hither, comrades, bring them one by one, these devils who could sit to watch a blind man walk to his doom to make their sport. Ah! whom have we here? Why, by Thor! 'tis the lawyer knave, he who was president of the court that tried you, and was angry because you did not salute him. Well, lawyer, the wheel has gone round. We Northmen are in possession of the palace and the Armenian legions are gathered at its gates and do but wait for Constantine the Emperor to enter and take the empire and its crown. They'll be here anon, lawyer, but you understand, having a certain life to save, for word had been brought to us of your pretty doings, that we were forced to strike before the signal, and struck not in vain. Now we'll fill in the tedious time with a trial of our own. See here, I am president of the court, seated in this fine chair, and these six to right and left are my companion judges, while you seven who were judges are now prisoners. You know the crime with which you are charged, so there's no need to set it out. Your defence, lawyer, and be swift with it."

"Oh! sir," said the man in a trembling voice, "what we did to the General Olaf we were ordered to do by one who may not be named."

"You'd best find the name, lawyer, for were it that of a god we Northmen would hear it."

"Well, then, by the Augusta herself. She wished the death of the noble Michael, or Olaf, but having become superstitious about the matter, would not have his blood directly on her hands. Therefore she bethought her of this plan. He was ordered to be brought into the place you see, which is known as the Hall of the Pit, that in old days was used by certain bloody-minded emperors to rid them of their enemies. The central pavement swings upon a hinge. At a touch it opens, and he who has thought it sound and walked thereon, when darkness comes is lost, since he falls upon the rocks far below, and at high tide the water takes him."

"Yes, yes, we understand the game, lawyer, for there yawns the open pit. But have you aught more to say?"

"Nothing, sir, nothing, save that we only did what we were driven to do. Moreover, no harm has come of it, since whenever the noble general came to the edge of the opened pit, although he was blind, he halted and went off to right or left as though someone drew him out of danger."

"Well, then, cruel and unjust judges, who could gather to mock at the murder of a blinded man that you had trapped to his doom——"

"Sir," broke in one of them, "it was not we who tried to trap him; it was those jailers who stand there. They told the general that he might exercise himself by walking up and down the hall."

"Is that true, Olaf?" asked Jodd.

"Yes," I answered, "it is true that the two jailers who brought me here did tell me this, though whether those men are present I cannot say."

"Very good," said Jodd. "Add them to the other prisoners, who by their own showing heard them set the snare and did not warn the victim. Now, murderers all, this is the sentence of the court upon you: That you salute the General Olaf and confess your wickedness to him."

So they saluted me, kneeling, and kissing my feet, and one and all made confession of their crime.

"Enough," I said, "I pardon them who are but tools. Pray to God that He may do as much."

"You may pardon here, Olaf," said Jodd, "and your God may pardon hereafter, but we, the Northmen, do not pardon. Blindfold those men and bind their arms. Now," went on Jodd after a pause, "their turn has come to show us sport. Run, friends, run, for swords are behind you. Can you not feel them?"

The rest may be guessed. Within a few minutes the seven judges and the two jailers had vanished from the world. No hand came to save *them* from the cruel rocks and the waters that seethed a hundred feet below that dreadful chamber.

This fantastic, savage vengeance was a thing dreadful to hear; what it must have been to see I can only guess. I know that I wished I might have fled from it and that I pleaded with Jodd for mercy on these men. But neither he nor his companions would listen to me.

"What mercy had they on you?" he cried. "Let them drink from their own cup."

"Let them drink from their own cup!" roared his companions, and then broke into a roar of laughter as one of the false judges, feeling space before him, leapt, leapt short, and with a shriek departed for ever.

It was over. I heard someone enter the hall and whisper in Jodd's ear; heard his answer also.

"Let her be brought hither," he said. "For the rest, bid the captains hold Stauracius and the others fast. If there is any sign of stir against us, cut their throats, advising them that this will be done should they allow trouble to arise. Do not fire the palace unless I give the word, for it would be a pity to burn so fine a building. It is those who dwell in it who should be burned; but doubtless Constantine will see to that. Collect the richest of the booty, that which is most portable, and let it be carried to our quarters in the baggage carts. See that these things are done quickly, before the Armenians get their hands into the bag. I'll be with you soon; but if the Emperor Constantine should arrive first, tell him that all has gone well, better than he hoped, indeed, and pray him to come hither, where we may take counsel."

The messenger went. Jodd and some of the Northmen began to consult together, and Martina led me aside.

"Tell me what has chanced, Martina," I asked, "for I am bewildered."

"A revolution, that is all, Olaf. Jodd and the Northmen are the point of the spear, its handle is Constantine, and the hands that hold it are the Armenians. It has been very well done. Some of the guards who remained were bribed, others frightened away. Only a few fought, and of them the Northmen made short work. Irene and her ministers were fooled. They thought the blow would not fall for a week or more, if at all, since the Empress believed that she had appeased Constantine by her promises. I'll tell you more later."

"How did you find me, Martina, and in time?"

"Oh! Olaf, it is a terrible story. Almost I swoon again to think of it. It was thus: Irene discovered that I had visited you in your cell; she grew suspicious of me. This morning I was seized and ordered to surrender the signet; but first I had heard that they planned your death to-day, not a sentence of banishment and murder afar off, as I told you. My last act before I was taken was to dispatch a trusted messenger to Jodd and the Northmen, telling them that if they would save you alive they must strike at once, and not to-night, as had been arranged. Within thirty seconds after he had left my side the eunuchs had me and took me to my chamber, where they barred me in. A while later the Augusta came raging like a lioness. She accused me of treachery, and when I denied it struck me in the face. Look, here are the marks of the jewels on her hands. Oh, alas! what said I? You cannot see. She had learned that the lady Heliodore had escaped her, and that I had some hand in her escape. She vowed that I, your god-mother, was your lover, and as this is a crime against the Church, promised me that after other sufferings I should be burned alive in the Hippodrome before all the people. Lastly she said this, 'Know that your Olaf of whom you are so fond dies within an hour and thus: He will be taken to the Hall of the Pit and there given leave to walk till the judges come. Being blind, you may guess where he will walk. Before this door is unlocked again I tell you he'll be but a heap of splintered bones. Aye, you may start and weep; but save your tears for yourself,' and she called me a foul name. 'I have got you fast at length, you night-prowling cat, and God Himself cannot give you strength to stretch out your hand and guide this accursed Olaf from the edge of the Pit of Death.'

"'God alone knows what He can do, Augusta,' I answered, for the words seemed to be put into my lips.

"Then she cursed and struck me again, and so left me barred in my chamber.

"When she had gone I flung myself upon my knees and prayed to God to save you, Olaf, since I was helpless; prayed as I had never prayed before. Praying thus, I think that I fell into a swoon, for my agony was more than I could bear, and in the swoon I dreamed. I dreamed that I stood in this place, where till now I have never been before. I saw the judges, the jailers, and a few others watching from that gallery. I saw you walk along the hall towards the great open pit. Then I seemed to glide to you and take your hand and guide you round the pit. And, Olaf, this happened thrice. Afterwards came a tumult while you were on the very edge of the pit and I held you, not suffering you to stir. Then in rushed the Northmen and I with them. Yes, standing there with you upon the edge of the pit, I saw myself and the Northmen rush into the hall."

"Martina," I whispered, "a hand that seemed to be a woman's did guide me thrice round the edge of the pit, and did hold me almost until you and the Northmen rushed in."

"Oh! God is great!" she gasped. "God is very great, and to Him I give thanks. But hearken to the end of the tale. I awoke from my swoon and heard noise without, and above it the Northmen's cry of victory. They had scaled the palace walls or broken in the gates—as yet I know not which— they were on the terrace driving the Greek guards before them. I ran to the window-place and there below me saw Jodd. I screamed till he heard me.

"'Save me if you would save Olaf,' I cried. 'I am prisoned here.'

"They brought one of their scaling ladders and drew me through the window. I told them all I knew. They caught a palace eunuch and beat him till he promised to lead us to this hall. He led, but in the labyrinth of passages fell down senseless, for they had struck him too hard. We knew not which way to turn, till suddenly we heard your voice and ran towards it.

"That is all the story, Olaf."

CHAPTER X
OLAF GIVES JUDGMENT

As Martina finished speaking I heard the sound of tramping guards and of a woman's dress upon the pavement. Then a voice, that of Irene, spoke, and though her words were quiet I caught in them the tremble of smothered rage.

"Be pleased to tell me, Captain Jodd," she said, "what is happening in my palace, and why I, the Empress, am haled from my apartment hither by soldiers under your command?"

"Lady," answered Jodd, "you are mistaken. Yesterday you were an empress, to-day you are—well, whatever your son, the Emperor, chooses to name you. As to what has been and is happening in this palace, I scarcely know where to begin the tale. First of all your general and chamberlain Olaf—in case you should not recognise him, I mean that blind man who stands yonder—was being tricked to death by certain servants of yours who called themselves judges, and who stated that they were acting by your orders."

"Confront me with them," said Irene, "that I may prove to you that they lie."

"Certainly. Ho! you, bring the lady Irene here. Now hold her over that hole. Nay, struggle not, lady, lest you should slip from their hands. Look down steadily, and you will see by the light that flows in from the cave beneath, certain heaps lying on the rocks round which the rising waters seethe. There are your judges whom you say you wish to meet. If you desire to ask them any questions, we can satisfy your will. Nay, why should you turn pale at the mere sight of the place that you thought good enough to be the bed of a faithful soldier of your own, one high in your service, whom it has pleased you to blind? Why did it please you to blind him, Lady?"

"Who are you that dare to ask me questions?" she replied, gathering up her courage.

"I'll tell you, Lady. Now that the General Olaf yonder is blinded I am the officer in command of the Northmen, who, until you tried to murder the said General Olaf a while ago, were your faithful guard. I am also, as it chances, the officer in command of this palace, which we took this morning by assault and by arrangement with most of your Greek soldiers, having learned from your confidential lady, Martina, of the vile deed you were about to work on the General Olaf."

"So it was you who betrayed me, Martina," gasped Irene; "and I had you in my power. Oh! I had you in my power!"

"I did not betray you, Augusta. I saved my god-son yonder from torture and butchery, as by my oath I was bound to do," answered Martina.

"Have done with this talk of betrayals," went on Jodd, "for who can betray a devil? Now, Lady, with your State quarrels we have nothing to do. You can settle them presently with your son, that is, if you still live. But with this matter of Olaf we have much to do, and we will settle that at once. The first part of the business we all know, so let us get to the next. By whose order were you blinded, General Olaf?"

"By that of the Augusta," I answered.

"For what reason, General Olaf?"

"For one that I will not state," I answered.

"Good. You were blinded by the Augusta for a reason you will not state, but which is well known to all of us. Now, we have a law in the North which says that an eye should be given for an eye and a life for a life. Would it not then be right, comrades, that this woman should be blinded also?"

"What!" screamed Irene, "blinded! I blinded! I, the Empress!"

"Tell me, Lady, are the eyes of one who was an Empress different from other eyes? Why should you complain of that darkness into which you were so ready to plunge one better than yourself. Still, Olaf shall judge. Is it your will, General, that we blind this woman who put out your eyes and afterwards tried to murder you?"

Now, I felt that all in that place were watching me and hanging on the words that I should speak, so intently that they never heard others entering it, as I did. For a while I paused, for why should not Irene suffer a little of that agony of suspense which she had inflicted upon me and others?

Then I said, "See what I have lost, friends, through no grave fault of my own. I was in the way of greatness. I was a soldier whom you trusted and liked well, one of unstained honour and of unstained name. Also I loved a woman, by whom I was beloved and whom I hoped to make my wife. And now what am I? My trade is gone, for how can a maimed man lead in war, or even do the meanest service of the camp? The rest of my days, should any be granted to me, must be spent in darkness blacker than that of midnight. I must live on charity. When the little store I have is spent, for I have taken no bribe and heaped up no riches, how can I earn a living? The woman whom I love has been carried away, after this Empress tried thrice to murder her. Whether I shall ever find her again in this world I know not, for she has gone to a far country that is full of enemies to Christian men. Nor do I know whether she would be willing to take one who is blind and beggared for a husband, though I think this may be so."

"Shame on her if she does not," muttered Martina as I paused.

"Well, friends, that is my case," I went on; "let the Augusta deny it if she can."

"Speak, Lady. Do you deny it?" said Jodd.

"I do not deny that this man was blinded by my order in payment of crimes for which he might well have suffered death," answered Irene. "But I do deny that I commanded him to be trapped in yonder pit. If those dead men said so, then they lied."

"And if the lady Martina says so, what then?" asked Jodd.

"Then she lies also," answered the Empress sullenly.

"Be it so," replied Jodd. "Yet it is strange that, acting on this lie of the lady Martina's, we found the General Olaf upon the very edge of yonder hole; yes, with not the breadth of a barleycorn between him and death. Now, General, both parties have been heard and you shall pass sentence. If you say that yonder woman is to be blinded, this moment she looks her last upon the light. If you say that she is to die, this moment she bids farewell to life."

Again I thought a while. It came into my mind that Irene, who had fallen from power, might rise once more and bring fresh evil upon Heliodore. Now she was in my hand, but if I opened that hand and let her free— —!

Someone moved towards me, and I heard Irene's voice whispering in my ear.

"Olaf," she said, "if I sinned against you it was because I loved you. Would you be avenged upon one who has burned her soul with so much evil because she loved too well? Oh! if so, you are no longer Olaf. For Christ's sake have pity on me, since I am not fit to meet Him. Give me time to repent. Nay! hear me out! Let not those men drag me away as they threaten to do. I am fallen now, but who knows, I may grow great again; indeed, I think I shall. Then, Olaf, may my soul shrivel everlastingly in hell if I try to harm you or the Egyptian more—Jesus be my witness that I ask no lesser doom upon my head. Keep the men back, Martina, for what I swear to him and the Egyptian I swear to you as well. Moreover, Olaf, I have great wealth. You spoke of poverty; it shall be far from you. Martina knows where my gold is hid, and she still holds my keys. Let her take it. I say leave me alone, but one word more. If ever it is in my power I'll forget everything and advance you all to great honour. Your brain is not blinded, Olaf; you can still rule. I swear, I swear, I swear upon the Holy Blood! Ah! now drag me away if you will. I have spoken."

"Then perchance, Lady, you will allow Olaf to speak, since we, who have much to do, must finish this business quickly, before the Emperor comes with the Armenians," said Jodd.

"Captain Jodd and his comrades," I said, "the Empress Irene has been pleased to make certain solemn vows to me which perchance some of you may have overheard. At least, God heard them, and whether she keeps them or no is a matter between her and the God in Whom we both believe. Therefore I set these vows aside; they draw me neither one way nor the other. Now, you have made me judge in my own matter and have promised to abide by my judgment, which you will do. Hear it, then, and let it be remembered. For long I have been the Augusta's officer, and of late her general and chamberlain. As such I have bound myself by great oaths to protect her from harm in all cases, and those oaths heretofore I have kept, when I might have broken them and not been blamed by men. Whatever has chanced, it seems that she is still Empress and I am still her officer, seeing that my sword has been returned to me, although it is true she sent it that I might use it on myself. It pleased the Empress to put out my eyes. Under our soldier's law the monarch who rules the Empire has a right to put out the eyes of an officer who has lifted sword against her forces, or even to kill him. Whether this is done justly or unjustly again is a matter between that monarch and God above, to Whom answer must be made at last. Therefore it would seem that I have no right to pronounce any sentence against the Augusta Irene, and whatever may have been my private wrongs, I pronounce none. Yet, as I am still your general until another is named, I order you to free the Augusta Irene and to work no vengeance on her person for aught that may have befallen me at her hands, were her deeds just or unjust."

When I had finished speaking, in the silence that followed I heard Irene utter something that was half a sob and half a gasp of wonderment. Then above the murmuring of the Northmen, to whom this rede was strange, rose the great voice of Jodd.

"General Olaf," he said, "while you were talking it came into my mind that one of those knife points which pierced your eyes had pricked the brain behind them. But when you had finished talking it came into my mind that you are a great man who, putting aside your private rights and wrongs and the glory of revenge which lay to your hand, have taught us soldiers a lesson in duty which I, at least, never shall forget. General, if, as I trust, we are together in the future as in the past, I shall ask you to instruct me in this Christian faith of yours, which can make a man not only forgive but hide his forgiveness under the mask of duty, for that, as we know well, is what you have done. General, your order shall be obeyed. Be she Empress or nothing, this lady's person is safe from us. More, we will protect her to the best of our power, as you did in the Battle of the Garden. Yet I tell her to her face that had it not been for those orders, had you, for example, said that you left judgment to us, she who has spoilt such a man should have died a death of shame."

I heard a sound as of a woman throwing herself upon her knees before me. I heard Irene's voice whisper through her tears,

"Olaf, Olaf, for the second time in my life you make me feel ashamed. Oh! if only you could have loved me! Then I should have grown good like you."

There was a stir of feet and another voice spoke, a voice that should have been clear and youthful, but sounded as though it were thick with wine. It did not need Martina's whisper to tell me that it was that of Constantine.

"Greeting, friends," he said, and at once there came a rattle of saluting swords and an answering cry of

"Greeting, Augustus!"

"You struck before the time," went on the thick, boyish voice. "Yet as things seem to have gone rather well for us, I cannot blame you, especially as I see that you hold fast her who has usurped my birthright."

Now I heard Irene turn with a swift and furious movement.

"Your birthright, boy," she cried. "What birthright have you save that which my body gave?"

"I thought that my father had more to do with this matter of imperial right than the Grecian girl whom it pleased him to marry for her fair face," answered Constantine insolently, adding: "Learn your station, mother. Learn that you are but the lamp which once held the holy oil, and that lamps can be shattered."

"Aye," she answered, "and oil can be spilt for the dogs to lap, if their gorge does not rise at such rancid stuff. The holy oil forsooth! Nay, the sour dregs of wine jars, the outscourings of the stews, the filth of the stables, of such is the holy oil that burns in Constantine, the drunkard and the liar."

It would seem that before this torrent of coarse invective Constantine quailed, who at heart always feared his mother, and I think never more so than when he appeared to triumph over her. Or perhaps he scorned to answer it. At least, addressing Jodd, he said,

"Captain, I and my officers, standing yonder unseen, have heard something of what passed in this place. By what warrant do you and your company take upon yourselves to pass judgment upon this mother of mine? That is the Emperor's right."

"By the warrant of capture, Augustus," answered Jodd. "We Northmen took the palace and opened the gates to you and your Armenians. Also we took her who ruled in the palace, with whom we had a private score to settle that has to do with our general who stands yonder, blinded. Well, it is settled in his own fashion, and now we do not yield up this woman, our prisoner, save on your royal promise that no harm shall come to her in body. As for the rest, it is your business. Make a cook-maid of her if you will, only then I think her tongue would clear the kitchen. But swear to keep her sound in life and limb till hell calls her, since otherwise we must add her to our company, which will make no man merrier."

"No," answered Constantine, "in a week she would corrupt you every one and breed a war. Well," he added with a boisterous laugh, "I'm master now at last, and I'll swear by any saint that you may name, or all of them, no harm shall come to this Empress whose rule is done, and who, being without friends, need not be feared. Still, lest she should spawn more mischief or murder, she must be kept close till we and our councillors decide where she shall dwell in future. Ho! guards, take my royal father's widow to the dower-palace, and there watch her well. If she escapes, you shall die beneath the rods. Away with the snake before it begins to hiss again."

"I'll hiss no more," said Irene, as the soldiers formed up round her, "yet, perchance, Constantine, you may live to find that the snake still has strength to strike and poison in its fangs, you and others. Do you come with me, Martina?"

"Nay, Lady, since here stands one whom God and you together have given me to guard. For his sake I would keep my life in me," and she touched me on the shoulder.

"That whelp who is called my son spoke truly when he said that the fallen have no friends," exclaimed Irene. "Well, you should thank me, Martina, who made Olaf blind, since, being without eyes, he cannot see how ugly is your face. In his darkness he may perchance mistake you for the beauteous Egyptian, Heliodore, as I know you who love him madly would have him do."

With this vile taunt she went.

"I think I'm crazed," said the Emperor, as the doors swung to behind her. "I should have struck that snake while the stick is in my hand. I tell you I fear her fangs. Why, if she could, she'd make me as that poor man is, blind, or even butcher me. Well, she's my mother, and I've sworn, so there's an end. Now, you Olaf, you are that same captain, are you not, who dashed the poisoned fig from my lips that this tender mother of mine would have let me eat when I was in liquor; yes, and would have swallowed it yourself to save me from my folly?"

"I am that man, Augustus."

"Aye, you are that man, and one of whom all the city has been talking. They say, so poor is your taste, that you turned your back upon the favours of an Empress because of some young girl you dared to love. They say also that she paid you back with a dagger in the eyes, she who was ready to set you in my place."

"Rumour has many tongues, Augustus," I answered. "At least I fell from the Empress's favour, and she rewarded me as she held that I deserved."

"So it seems. Christ! what a dreadful pit is that. Is this another of her gifts? Nay, answer not; I heard the tale. Well, Olaf, you saved my life and your Northmen have set me on the throne, since without them we could scarcely have won the palace. Now, what payment would you have?"

"Leave to go hence, Augustus," I answered.

"A small boon that you might have taken without asking, if you can find a dog to lead you, like other blind wretches. And you, Captain Jodd, and your men, what do you ask?"

"Such donation as it may please the Augustus to bestow, and after that permission to follow wherever our General Olaf goes, since he is our care. Here we have made so many enemies that we cannot sleep at night."

"The Empress of the World falls from her throne," mused Constantine, "and not even a waiting-maid attends her to her prison. But a blinded captain finds a regiment to escort him hence in love and honour, as though he were a new-crowned king. Truly Fortune is a jester. If ever Fate should rob me of my eyes, I wonder, when I had nothing more to give them, if three hundred faithful swords would follow me to ruin and to exile?"

Thus he thought aloud. Afterwards he, Jodd and some others, Martina among them, went aside, leaving me seated on a bench. Presently they returned, and Constantine said,

"General Olaf, I and your companions have taken counsel. Listen. But to-day messengers have come from Lesbos, whom we met outside the gates. It seems that the governor there is dead, and that the accursed Moslems threaten to storm the isle as soon as summer comes and add it to their empire. Our Christian subjects there pray that a new governor may be appointed, one who knows war, and that with him may be sent troops sufficient to repel the prophet-worshippers, who, not having many ships, cannot attack in great force. Now, Captain Jodd thinks this task will be to the liking of the Northmen, and though you are blind, I think that you would serve me well as governor of Lesbos. Is it your pleasure to accept this office?"

"Aye, with thankfulness, Augustus," I answered. "Only, after the Moslems are beaten back, if it pleases God that it should so befall, I ask leave of absence for a while, since there is one for whom I must search."

"I grant it, who name Captain Jodd your deputy. Stay, there's one more thing. In Lesbos my mother has large vineyards and estates. As part payment of her debt these shall be conveyed to you. Nay, no thanks; it is I who owe them. Whatever his faults, Constantine is not ungrateful. Moreover, enough time has been spent upon this matter. What say you, Officer? That the Armenians are marshalled and that you have Stauracius safe? Good! I come to lead them. Then to the Hippodrome to be proclaimed."